CW00857889

ESEGI'S MIND
AND OTHER STORIES

Gesiere Brisibe-Dorgu

authorHOUSE®

AuthorHouse™
1663 Liberty Drive
Bloomington, IN 47403
www.authorhouse.com
Phone: 1 (800) 839-8640

Published by AuthorHouse 03/29/2018

ISBN: 978-1-5462-3600-9 (sc)
ISBN: 978-1-5462-3599-6 (hc)
ISBN: 978-1-5462-3598-9 (e)

Library of Congress Control Number: 2018903914

Print information available on the last page.

Any people depicted in stock imagery provided by Getty Images are models,
and such images are being used for illustrative purposes only.
Certain stock imagery © Getty Images.

This book is printed on acid-free paper.

Because of the dynamic nature of the Internet, any web addresses or links contained in
this book may have changed since publication and may no longer be valid. The views
expressed in this work are solely those of the author and do not necessarily reflect the
views of the publisher, and the publisher hereby disclaims any responsibility for them.

Contents

Contents

DEDICATED

To all the wonderful storytellers with whom I have interacted over the years, thank you very much!

This book would not have been possible without your generous contributions.

ESEGI'S MIND

The first thing people noticed on meeting this unique individual were his eyeballs. They protruded forcefully from their sockets.

"What an usual shape of head!" people would comment.

"It is like an avocado pear of many sides! Why does he stiffen his arms when he walks, making them look like lifeless objects attached to a mannequin?" they would whisper.

However, when he smiled, his immaculate white teeth always attracted favourable comments. With a respectable height of about four feet, this simple man called ESEGI lived a fairly contented life. His philosophy of life was as simple as the man himself. He was fond of repeating a profound statement he credited to his mother.

"My Mama used to say to me, Esegi-O! A person who has a good teacher, can never go astray and he who asks for directions when not sure, never gets lost."

Esegi took the above advice so much to heart that he made it his life's creed, though in a special way. He always asked other people to either interpret or explain every question that was put to him or about anything he wanted to do. His most ardent adviser, a person with the slow movements of a snail and a neck so firmly wedged between his shoulder blades that head and shoulders were almost joined. This adviser was none other than the famous EWIRI. He was also Esegi's bosom friend of many years and the two were practically inseparable. Esegi would occasionally sigh and wonder out loud.

"What in Ewiri's brain makes him so brilliant? How could someone, who is so ugly that children run away at the sight of him be even wiser than our fat, tall and thoughtful *Amanana-owei*? Mm!" He would muse, silently vowing not to open his mouth without clarification from his dear friend.

One fine morning, during the dry season when the harmattan winds were at their height, Esegi, still wrapped in his 'cover cloth,' decided to cross to the opposite side of the stream separating the village from the farmlands. It was just a few feet wide and people on either side conversed without strain. He called to his fair complexioned plump wife Alabata who was already on the other side. Though she was warming herself by a small fire, he wanted her to come over and ferry him across. She asked if he was alone and characteristically he did not answer her immediately, having not consulted his chief adviser Ewiri, who luckily was with him. He turned to his friend and asked,

"What do you think she means by asking if I am alone?"

"What she means is not a mystery, friend. All she's saying is that you should return home to pick up some items that would be of interest to her, including a boat," responded Ewiri.

Esegi immediately left for his house, telling Alabata at the top of his voice.

"I am running home to do your bidding without delay my sweet wife!"

Alabata though confused, responded that she would wait for him.

"Hurry up-O! I have a lot to do in the farm and will start clearing the bush as soon as I have warmed myself well enough," she responded.

Esegi again asked Ewiri for clarification of his wife's response.

"Alabata wants you to go for the items all by yourself. She does not want you to go along with any friend and she says you should be quick about it."

Esegi embraced his friend's waist, thanked him and ran home.

As soon as he left, Ewiri called out to Alabata.

"A'a-a Alabata! Your husband says you should immediately come and meet me for some secret instructions."

"He-ee! Ewiri! Are you sure that was what my husband told you? One can never be sure about..."

"Yes of course! Do I look like a liar, en! Am I not your husband's best friend?" Ewiri retorted indignantly.

Satisfied that he must be telling the truth, she paddled across to meet him.

When they met, Ewiri confided that her husband was actually a very dangerous man who had sinister plans. He therefore assured her that Esegi was not the type of man for a hardworking woman like her. Many more damaging things were revealed which convinced her of Ewiri's sincerity. Alabata was very impressed with the way he reasoned and vowed to deal with her husband. Upon his return, Esegi met a very hostile and angry Alabata.

"I didn't know you were such a wicked man Esegi!" She shouted angrily.

"Anyway, thank God Ewiri had the good sense to reveal all the little secrets you told him. You even went as far as telling him to marry me! I can never understand why my own husband will tell his friend to marry me. This is senseless but I am glad you said so. Yes, I will marry him! I am sure he will make a better husband than you. Foolish man!" she fumed.

"What is she talking about?" A perplexed Esegi asked his friend.

Ewiri stroked his moustache and was not forthcoming.

"Aboo Ewiri, please tell me if you understand what my wife saying."

"Err..I think she means that she prefers to marry me but abeg, don't ask me why she is saying such a thing. I prefer that you settle that between yourselves." He said, looking at a set of butterflies perched on a cocoyam leaf, while still stroking his moustache.

At this point, Esegi became utterly confused. He scratched his head and looked upwards, then down. He felt like laughing and crying all at the same time! He did not quite know whether the emotion he was experiencing was that of betrayal, fear or anger. On the other hand, his friend Ewiri appeared more interested in looking at the many lizards and frogs scouring around for food. Esegi was disappointed in his wife for suddenly abandoning him. The trauma was almost too much for him to bear. For the first time in his life, he was forced to think for himself, albeit momentarily. He decided to appeal to his wife directly.

"Alabata my beloved wife, why are you talking of leaving me for this useless, ugly Ewiri, hnn? He is short, has no neck and won't even be able to walk fast enough to catch up with a long-legged beauty like you. A millipede is a racing dog compared to him! Why then attach yourself to such a person? " He asked in a caressing tone.

Alabata was very surprised that Esegi could ask her such a question after all the humiliation she had suffered.

"I cannot believe my ears!" she screamed.

"Did you not see his ugliness before telling him to tell me to marry him, because you have found a more beautiful woman than me? So why are you now questioning me? Look, I know you have a head that has three bulges like Mama Tare's *akpu* but surely, your brain too cannot be out of shape?"

At this point, Esegi became totally discouraged and lapsed into his old mind-set. He reluctantly turned to Ewiri and sought explanation of what Alabata had just said.

"*Abeg* Ewiri, I still consider you a friend. Do not abandon me." He pleaded.

"Can you explain in detail, what my wife is trying to tell me?"

"With pleasure!" responded Ewiri smiling.

"What Alabata means is this," he began, then paused and started removing some invisible particles from his head. Esegi was getting impatient and started fidgeting.

"*Ewiri, sisei gbaa!*" He appealed, almost tearfully.

"Look at Alabata very well, will you?" Ewiri ordered.

"Yes, yes! I am looking at her now," nodded a slightly hopeful but baffled Esegi.

The extra strain of opening his eyes wide produced reddish spots in the man's distended eyeballs.

"She is a very beautiful woman and one would have thought that eyes as big as yours, will see beyond her outer beauty which…"

"Hey, hold on!" Esegi interrupted, now completely lost. He pointed a finger at his wife, who was still standing at the opposite bank of the narrow stream.

"Explain what you mean by what you just said and also what Alabata said last time."

"Okay then!" Ewiri said with a determined nod.

"What I mean is this. A woman like Alabata, is special. Her inner beauty is even greater than the outer one. That is the precise reason for the confusion she is causing in the hearts of many men. As for the meaning of what she said, it is simple. You should go to the market place and tell any old woman you find to come and beg her for you, then…"

Even before Ewiri finished speaking, Esegi was already running.

"Aha-aa!" he exclaimed.

"I knew she would make such a request. That is my Alabata speaking! My lovely wife, I love you-ayy! Thank you Ewiri! I will go about the assignment immediately!"

He sped off to the market without a backward glance, tripping and falling in the process, as his feet got entangled in some palm fronds.

'Nasty palms!' He murmured. 'You think you can stop me? No way! I must come back with an old woman to beg my beloved Alabata. Yes! She will then smile, sing and dance for Esegi, her husband forever!

<u>**GLOSSARY**</u>

Abeg	-	*Pidgin please*
Akpu	-	*Cassava flour meal*
Amanana-owei	-	*Traditional ruler of a town/village*
Sisei gbaa	-	*Please say it*

THE EKINE PRIEST

Many cultures believe that the creator of the world always provide intercessors for mankind in the form of unseen but felt deities. The advent of Christianity and Islam in West Africa has however, changed attitudes to some extent. While some communities embraced the new religions with enthusiasm, others were slow in incorporating it into their daily lives. The Niger Delta region of Nigeria is one such place, where change has been slow. Many call themselves Christians but still fear the unseen deities or forces. A number of communities still respect the intercessory deities and actively worship them. We are going to meet one man who took his job as custodian of one such deity EKINE, very, very seriously.

"A-a-boo! The clouds frown when he is angry! Lightening warns before he sets foot in his battle canoe and thunder shakes everywhere when he raises his head!"

The above statement was made by the *Bebe-are-owei* of Ekine-ama, when a stranger asked him to describe the Ekine priest.

"What about rain? Does it not follow the great priest? I was told that…."

"A-aa!" The *Bebe-are-owei* interrupted the stranger.

"When the Ekine priest asks the rain to dress the earth with showers, all in the vicinity run to hide. What comes with the rain is not for ordinary eyes. My sister, the mere mention of Ekine's rain makes my body shake."

"But why are his eyes always bloodshot and…"

"Please, please let us discuss something else," he pleaded, frowning slightly.

High Priest Karekarebo, embodied all the attributes of the Ekine deity. He alone occupies the inner chambers of the Ekine shrine. The outer spacious room, usually open to all, looked like a scene from a horror movie. Blood stained palm fronds, animal and fish related ornaments and two red and yellow carved giants, adorned the four corners. It was the duty of the High Priest to present the human face of Ekine and he did this by organizing colourful masquerade festivals once a year.

Karekarebo was as short as a tree trunk, with a belly that was round and distended. His shining baldhead adorned a thick neck. This respected priest customarily wore dresses highlighting the deity's colours of orange, red, black and blue. A two-feet high straw hat made of birds' feathers, completed the regalia. His face would usually be painted in four equal parts of red, black, orange and blue. He was awe-inspiring and few dared look him in the eye. The man was even reputed to have the capacity to transform himself into beast, reptile, tree, water or any other material he so desired. With its legendary reputation for dealing decisively with guilty persons, the Ekine deity was revered and feared by both adherents and non-adherents alike.

One fine morning, when the sun came out early to greet its children and the tide was high, the High Priest visited his good friend Amatare.

"I am thinking of visiting the forest to a brief interaction with our friends in that kingdom. Would you like to join me? What say you my friend?" He asked.

"Haa! No need to ask twice. You know I can never pass up an opportunity to show my hunting skills!"

"Very well then. We shall see who the better hunter will be, this time!"

Amatare was excited at the prospect of a lively expedition with his friend. After a breakfast of steaming fresh fish *beribe okodo*, they paddled leisurely down the river. Counting the water lotuses floating by was a practice they enjoyed, right from their childhood days, while cheerfully greeting the women on their way to farmlands or fishponds. They waved to some men standing by the riverbank.

"A-doo! A-nua-O!"

Suddenly, the priest turned to his friend.

"Amatare, we must make a brief stop at the burial ground. It is very important that we do so immediately!"

"Apoo- iye! That was not the plan. I refuse to listen to you this time. *Benebene*! I am not going to any burial ground when there is no corpse to bury!" Amatare protested.

In a tone that sounded like the beat of a gong, the priest spoke calmly and deliberately.

"I shall point my finger to a particular spot and that's where you will anchor the canoe!"

Like a stubborn child subdued by a parent's threat, Amatare nodded.

Shortly thereafter, they anchored and went ashore.

The priest moved swiftly into the dense forest, closely followed by a hesitant Amatare. They walked in silence for about fifteen minutes, then Karekarebo stopped abruptly. He quickly pulled out his cutlass from its holster and cut the grass around an area, about seven feet in diameter. Thereafter, he drew two circles with white chalk and told his bemused friend to occupy one of the circles, while he got into the other. He further instructed Amatare to be calm and not to be afraid, no matter what happened.

"Fear will attract unpleasant consequences." He stressed.

"Hm! I hear you *iye!* A blind man knows when it's harmattan by the harshness of the wind blowing against his face," Amatare replied.

"Just observe events without displaying any emotion," Karekarebo advised.

Amatare nodded, not trusting himself to speak.

Then as he looked on, Karekarebo, laid on the ground and stretched until he became as stiff as a dead body. All breathing ceased completely. The body started to swell until it became so bloated that it bust open at several places spewing worms, pus and blood mixed with water! The circle he occupied was now overflowing with a mixture of all the above in a messy slimy pool. The stench was unbearable but Amatare remained calm. Only his luminous eyes, betrayed the anxiety he felt inside. As all this was going on, the ground suddenly split open and Karekarebo's entire body was swallowed up!

At that very moment, a huge python moved into Amatare's circle, wrapped its slippery self around the man's feet and started leaking his hands and feet. He did not flinch but his body was as rigid as a concrete electric pole. After a while though, the python slithered away, only to be replaced by a horde of mosquitoes. They covered every inch of his body, buzzing merrily. Their 'visit' was only momentary, paving way for two teenage white boys! White boys, appearing in the dense jungle of *Izon-ebe*! Amatare must have been astonished beyond words but then, who wouldn't? The duo proceeded to present him with a note pad and pen in a ceremonious manner. Just as he was telling himself that the boys certainly did not know he was a functional illiterate, the power of literacy was instantly conferred on him. He was asked to write down everything that was dictated by them. The boys also showed him all manner of herbs and roots and their uses. The 'lecture' continued for several hours. Then, as suddenly as they appeared, the boys disappeared!

As if by signal, the ground opened with a roaring sound and standing before him was Ekine Priest Karekarebo, in full regalia! He had a secret smile on his face. Words were unnecessary. The two friends merely nodded at each other and quietly continued their journey.

Amatare eventually became the greatest healer of his day. Needless to say his incredible knowledge of herbs and his ability to heal even the 'incurables' was a surprise to many and debates about how he acquired these gifts continue to this day.

GLOSSARY

A-a-boo	-	*Expression of awe or surprise*
A-do! A-nua!	-	*General greeting (plural)*
Benebene	-	*Never*
Apoo! Iye	-	*Hey, friend.*
Izon-ebe	-	*Izon(Ijaw) Nationality*
Beribe Okodo	-	*Traditional meal cooked with unripe plantain*

THE GOLDEN BIRD

Toke-ere was tall, willowy and born dumb, while her sister Ebi-ere was short, beautiful, outgoing and had all her senses intact. Together with their parents, they lived in a three-room mud house, plastered with cement. The family had a highly treasured gold coloured pet bird, which was kept in a tiny bamboo cage in the centre of their living room.

Whenever the parents left home, Ebi-ere would let the bird out of its cage and allow it fly all over the place. After a while, she would call it back with a song.

"Dee ofoni korobo atangbala-ange fe!" and it would happily fly back and eat rice out of her palm.

But one morning, while the golden bird was out playing, it saw other golden birds and flew away with them. Ebi-ere sang its song several times but there was no sign of the bird. No matter how sweetly she sang, it refused to come back. When it dawned on her that the bird had flown away for good, she was horrified. Crying loudly, she ran into the kitchen situated behind the main house. Once there, she crawled into a corner of the fireplace, scooped a handful of ash and rubbed it all over her body. Toke-ere, who had followed her sister and witnessed the rubbing of ash frowned and made a sign asking,

"What is the matter with you? Why are you sitting by the fire place with ash all over your body?"

"Listen carefully!" Ebi-ere told her sister sternly.

"When our parents return and ask of me, tell them that I have gone out. Do you hear me?" She asked, pulling her ears for effect. Toke-ere nodded, unsure of her sister's motives.

When the parents returned home in the evening and did not see Ebi-ere, they asked Toke-ere where her sister was. She at first pretended not to hear them. However, when her father asked again in a voice that sounded like the boom of Gbosa, the village musician's drum, she nervously pointed to the fireplace. The surprised parents did not know what to make of Ebi-ere's behaviour.

"What is the meaning of this?" They asked almost simultaneously. Ebi-ere stood up shakily, tears streaming down her face.

"O Daada! Naana! The golden bird has flown away! I did not do it deliberately. Please forgive me. *Sisei* I..."

"You did what?" Thundered her father, eyes closed.

"Are you telling me a story or has my golden bird really gone?"

"Eee Daada! I was only playing with the bird. I didn't know it......"

"You foolish a-a-nd idiotic girl! How could you do this to us? You have destroyed us! You fool! Oh, my precious golden bird!" He lamented, tears trickling down his face.

The parents' anger was so great that they dragged the now wailing and pleading Ebiere to a secluded place and beat her until she became unconscious. Fearing that she may have died and not wanting inquisitive neighbours to know what was going on, they put her into a partially broken old canoe and hid it behind some elephant grasses at the bank of the river.

The canoe, with its unconscious occupant, was floating down the river when a high priestess out feeding her gods with sweet biscuits, discovered it. She was tempted to allow the canoe float by but changed her mind after inspecting its contents. Grim faced, she tied the canoe to hers and paddled

13

briskly. As soon as she got to shore, she carried the now apparently dead girl to her ordinary-looking mud house, situated at the extreme northern end of the village. With loving care, the priestess nursed Ebi-ere back to health and adopted her. She did not have a child of her own so this adopted daughter became the centre of her world.

Meanwhile, on a particular all-communities market day when the rain was falling heavily, Ebiere's parents thought they glimpsed someone like their 'dead' daughter but were not quite sure.

A few months after the first 'sighting,' they saw her again during a major market day. Being more certain this time, they decided to trail her. Stories abounded in and around their community about dead persons buying and selling among the living during big market days. They wanted to confirm if this was also the case with their 'dead' daughter. Their detective work took them to a surprising and unexpected place. It was the house of the reclusive and somewhat feared OSUOPELE high priestess! She came out to confront them, wearing her full ceremonial regalia of bright red, yellow and orange dress, complete with her trademark python skin headband.

"Why are you here?" she asked.

"We saw a girl that looked like our daughter, so we followed her. We thought she came to this house," they answered aggressively.

The priestess clenched her fists and in a voice that sounded like the bark of a dog, scolded the husband and wife.

"You have the courage to pursue somebody you have already killed and call her your own? Remember who I am. You have stepped into a beehive and you will be stung all over your body, if you do not go back to wherever it is you are coming from!

"Why are you angry? What is our offence?" They asked.

"We only want our daughter and your reaction tells us that she is here. Please bring her out!" They demanded.

"I cannot believe my ears!" The priestess shouted.

"How dare you frighten my precious daughter by following her? Have you no sense of shame, you stupid husband and wife?"

"Do not insult us because of our own daughter. How can you stand here and tell us..."

"Keep quiet and start running away from here before I lose my temper," the priestess ordered.

"So you are not satisfied with killing the poor child once? How can you even determine that your dead child still exists, tell me?"

"O! The girl we saw looked so much like our beloved Ebi-ere," they told her, nervously looking right and left.

"She is the only one we have left now. Our other daughter is now crippled and deaf, in addition to being born dumb. It is only Ebi-ere who can..."

The priestess finally lost her temper and pointed her magic rod at them.

"I shall turn you to mad monkeys immediately, if you do not leave this minute! *Saram!*"

They fled, protesting loudly and promising to be back.

Ebi-ere came out from her hiding place inside the shrine when she was sure the people had gone.

"Mother, why were they pursuing me? I did not offend anyone in the market. I was simply selling what you gave me and..."

"Ssh! My little one," the priestess admonished, smiling tenderly.

"Come sit by me and listen attentively to what I am about to tell you, *na?*"

"*Yin-yo* Mama!" Ebiere said, nodding vigorously.

"I was out feeding my gods in the river when a disused canoe floating by caught my attention. I wanted to allow the canoe go but my gods would not let me. So, I took the virtually dead person to my shrine. With the help of Otobotobo the healing spirit, the individual was made whole again!"

"What!" Exclaimed Ebi-ere.

"Mother, where is this person the gods brought back to life?"

"The person, my dearest child," replied the priestess.

"Is sitting by my side!"

"*Oyin-ma! Teyene*!" Screamed Ebie-ere.

"You mean I am... I mean, I was killed and..."

"Yes indeed!" the priestess answered holding the speechless girl to her bosom.

Ebiere's tears flowed unchecked, though she didn't know whether they were tears of joy, sadness or pity. Her adopted mother took her by the hand and walked her to the shrine and pointed to the spot where the 'miracle' took place. She told Ebi-ere that nobody was saw or knew about the incident because of the location of her house. She said mystical herbs, roots and incantations were the only things used to bring Ebi-ere back to life.

"Look at you my precious one! So beautiful, strong and wise! Growing more beautiful in my eyes everyday! Not a single scar on your body! Do you know my child, that all the young men in this village and beyond want your hand in marriage?"

"Oh! Mother!" Ebi-ere, now full of smiles protested shyly.

GLOSSARY

Aboo	-	*Exclamation of surprise or annoyance*
Dee ofoni korobo		
Atangbala-ange fe	-	*Watch bird, come down and eat rice.*
Na	-	*Do you hear (me)?*
Oyin-ma	-	*Dear mother God.*
Sisei	-	*Please.*
Teyene!	-	*What!*
Yin-yo	-	*Yes indeed!*

GOLD EVERYWHERE

There once lived an industrious man called Amunyai. He was tall, hairy, ebony black and handsome. Many parents brought their daughters for him to marry because he was simple, forthright and well-to-do. This notwithstanding, he decided to marry only four wives. His virility was not in doubt, as all four women usually got pregnant in sequence. They jostled to outdo each other in attracting his attention. When meals were prepared, the head of fish considered to be the most valuable part, was always reserved for him.

When the babies started arriving, some mothers grumbled that he did not transfer his good looks to their children. Amunyai always took delight in 'inspecting' his children when they are born, making interesting comments as he did so.

"Ha! This one will be a great hunter, I can tell by the strength of its grip! What a fine nose she has! I will make sure she marries an equally handsome man! *Aboo!* Tare-ere, where did these legs come from? I ought to have examined those legs of yours before paying the fat dowry your father demanded! Er-hnn! This is my carbon copy, *owei ke owei*! Very good, ha! ha!"

As his family grew, Amunyai thought it wise to establish a work camp some kilometres from his main community of OGBOSU. The camp was a happy place full of laughter and singing most evenings. Amunyai tapped palm wine and brewed gin with the assistance of his wives. Unlike other men of his day who considered it unmanly not beat a wife from time to time, Amunyai never brutalized any of his wives. In addition to the gin business, he also had a sizeable yam and plantain farm so there was always enough food to eat. People paddling by the camp usually commented on the sweet aroma of fish roasting in open fires. Amunyai would invite them to stop over.

"Ado-O! A'emi? Come down and have some roast fish and *ofonia* before paddling on," he would call out cheerfully.

"O! Thank you very much Amunyai. We are coming!" they would respond, jumping down from their canoes. After the usual embraces and a hearty meal, the guests would depart, full of gratitude.

"Oyin e'tare-O! Krotimi-O!" They would say.

Amunyai's camp expanded as the years went by. In obedience to the Creator's command to go out and multiply, his children became adults, got married and started their independent businesses. There were now grand children to pick out grey hairs from Amunyai's head as he told them fairy tales. He was a contented man and this was the situation of things until he suddenly fell gravely ill one rainy day.

His condition was so serious that the family, fearing that he might die any minute sent emissaries to members of their extended family in the parent community, Ogbosu. They felt that the proper thing was to have their husband and father buried in his hometown, in the event of his death. The messengers were well received by both extended family and townspeople. After a brief meeting, a selected group of elders were immediately mandated to accompany the emissaries to their camp, now known as AMUNYAI BOU.

Upon arrival, the group discovered that the old man was still alive, though he could no longer talk. Being experienced and conversant with the dying process, the elders knew that Pa Amunyai had very little time to live. They consulted among themselves and agreed that there was no need for them to go back immediately or move the sick man to Ogbosu, as one person suggested. It was unanimously agreed therefore, that they just keep vigil in the room until his final breath and thereafter, take the body to Ogbosu for burial. With little else to do, the men proceeded to make themselves comfortable around Amunyai's mud bed, drinking shots of local gin to keep their stomachs warm. As the night wore on, they started falling asleep one after another.

By the time they woke up the next morning, the body of Pa Amunyai was no longer visible! It was totally covered by an anthill! Even the oldest man Preye, who thought he had seen everything, was speechless.

"A-a-bo-o! A-a-bo-o!" He exclaimed.

"So, a man can bury himself ehhnn! Unheard off! Incredible! Impossible!"

"Nobody should boast about their experiences, when they have yet to go beyond the rainbow." Another elder remarked.

"Eh! It is they, who go out into the world that see strange things. What a day! What a man!" Commented Alibo, the great hunter.

Many were speechless and kept shaking their heads from side to side. Reasoning that there was nothing more for them to do since Pa Amunyai had decided to bury himself, they left for Ogbosu, speaking in low tones. As word of Pa Amunyai's self-burial spread, Amunyai Bou became an instant tourist attraction. People from far and near came to see the burial mound and went back to their homes, flabbergasted.

Many years later, some villagers farming near Amunyai's self-burial site, noticed some powdery substance like fine brown sand. It covered the entire grave and around it. Curious, they moved closer and saw that the dusty material was gold coloured. Being unsure of what the substance was, no one touched it. Upon further examination, the farmers discovered that a solid bar of gold-like object was also embedded on the spot where the body of late Amunyai was covered by the anthill. The phenomenon was strange enough for them to abandon their work for the day. They ran to the village square, shouting.

"Amunyai Bou! Amunyai Bou! A'boo! A'bo di-y-o-o-O!"

People started running towards the square, only to see others running in the opposite direction. Fearing that some calamity had befallen the community, young children started crying. Finally, the true story was circulated and every one trooped to the grave to behold the wonder. Nobody had an explanation for what they saw.

One hundred years after Pa Amunyai's call to the land of his ancestors, people from far and near continue to visit the gravesite to behold the golden wonder. Legend has it that only women are allowed to take care of this unique gravesite. Once a year, women of the community visit the grave and reverently gather all the gold dust. Thereafter, the entire site is swept and the gathered gold dust neatly arranged around the gold bar. The women would then offer prayers and leave.

This practice has continued unbroken, until today.

GLOSSARY

Aboo!	-	*Exclamation of surprise/irritation*
A-do-o!	-	*Greeting*
A'emi?	-	*How are you? (Plural)*
Krotimi-O	-	*Stay in good health/I wish you well*
Ofonia	-	*Sun-dried pieces of fermented cassva*
Owei ke owei	-	*A real man*
Tare-ere	-	*Beloved or favoured wife*

OTOU THE HUNTER

"Why is that man's right shoulder bent when he is not a hunchback?"

"Eey! What type of question is that? Do you have to be a hunchback to have a bent shoulder? I thought you would comment on his eyes, which always appear slanted as they look at people from head to toe, as if... one were an antelope in hiding, ready to be hunted down! He also bares his teeth and brings out his tongue like a dog about to eat a juicy bone! Ha! Ha! Ha! Make sure he does not hear you-O!"

The conversation above was between two young men and the object of their interchange was none other than OTOU, the great hunter.

A skilful and respected hunter, Otou was also known to be a very spiritual person. Many in his community wondered how someone in a violent profession like hunting could at the same time be spiritual. They could also not reconcile his stocky looks with his job. After all, hunters are supposed to be slim and fit, isn't it? Otou's barrel-shaped look notwithstanding, he was soft spoken, compassionate and smiled often.

Very early one misty morning, Otou, wearing a leopard skin shirt and with Dane gun slung over his shoulder, went deep into the forest. He alone knew that the mission he had assigned himself that day was a daunting one.

'Where others have failed, I will succeed.' He murmured, striding purposefully through narrow but familiar paths.

None of the experienced hunters in the land had succeeded in tracking down the famed one-eyed elephant, the object of his expedition that day. The leaves of the thick jungle's big trees and timber glistened with dew. All senses on full alert, the hunter's full attention was concentrated on his immediate environment. Then suddenly, he stood still.

'What is this I hear?' He whispered and listened more attentively.

'Yes! I can hear voices but who could be out here at this time? Is it possible for that braggart, Tentebe to have beaten me in the search? This will be disastrous for my reputation. Mm!' He mused.

Determined to identify the speakers, Otou stepped around some trees with the lightness of a fairy in order not to make any noise. Cautiously, he moved in the direction of the voices. He had barely moved four yards, when he saw an old woman and a young girl talking animatedly. He quickly hid behind a big tree. As he watched and listened, his amazement grew.

"You are to be born to one Ebikake and Gbekemo, who will shower you with love. However, as you grow up to become a beautiful teenager, you are to return to me." The old woman instructed.

"I will not fail to return to you my dearest mother. I will do as you ask. This is my promise and you know I keep my promises!" The girl responded brightly.

Otou could hardly believe his ears. He stood there long after the conversing pair had departed, oblivious to the movements of some monkeys high above the tree he was resting on.

He had heard from village gossips that Ebikake and Gbekemo, who lived in the neighbouring village, were still childless after many years of marriage because all children born to them had died in infancy. Now, another child was going to be born to them and he knew that this one too would die young. What was he to do? Losing all interest to hunt, he went back home. Suddenly, the all-important search for the elusive one-eyed elephant didn't seem so important anymore. His sole concern at the moment was the utilization of the information at his disposal for the benefit of the childless couple.

In the evening of that same day, Otou visited Ebikake and Gbekemo in their simple thatch-roofed house built on stilts of ironwood and bamboo floorboards. He introduced himself as a prophet and informed the husband and wife that they would soon become proud parents of another child. Continuing he said,

"If the child is a boy, he will be my friend and if a girl, she will be my wife. What do you say, Ebikake and Gbekemo? The surprised couple looked at each other and at the speaker.

"We do not know if you speak in the name of the gods but we accept what you have said because sincerity hides not its colours. Thank you!" Gbekemo said to 'prophet' Otou.

"According to our people, a sick person is the soothsayer's slave. We are sick for a child and if you say my wife is going to have another child, who are we to argue? Let it be as you have said and I join my wife to thank you!" Ebikake added. Otou was happy that the couple accepted his request.

A few months after the 'prophet's' visit, Gbekemo became pregnant. She did not tell her husband until two months into the pregnancy.

"Ahh Gbekemo! You should have told me immediately you suspected that…"

"O my husband, please do not be angry with me! I did not want to tempt fate by revealing my condition so early…"

"But Gbekemo, the prophet has already prophesied that this child will stay.

"I know he said so but one cannot be careful enough. Anyway, now you know! I will like us to keep things to ourselves until…"

"You are right about that. I totally agree that people should only hear about the child after he or she is born."

This pregnancy turned out to be quite different from her previous ones. While all her former children were usually in a hurry to come to the world, not lasting up to nine months in their mother's womb, this particular child did not get delivered until the eleventh month! When the traditional midwife announced that the child was a girl, Ebikake was a bit disappointed. He had hoped for a boy with whom he would go hunting, farming and above all, hand over his gin brewing business to. All these were fleeting thoughts and were not allowed to dampen the joy of the moment.

"Is she not beautiful?" Gbekemo asked as Ebikake came in to greet her.

"She is so beautiful, just like a little goddess! Well-done my wife!"

The happy parents sent a trusted friend to inform Otou about the safe birth of his 'wife.'

"O! A girl you say?

"This is a happy day!" He exclaimed.

The vindicated 'prophet' immediately jumped into his small canoe and paddled excitedly to the home of the new parents, bearing gifts for the new-born.

"I am going to keep an eye on you my angelic infant bride," he teased, patting the baby's rosy cheeks. Everyone laughed.

The child grew up fast and was proclaimed to be the most beautiful girl in the entire clan. A lot more was said about this mysterious looking young girl.

"She is so tall and beautiful! How could she have been borne by Ebikake and Gbekemo, who are both short and dark complexioned?"

"Desperate people go to strange lengths in their search for a child and who knows where those two got their so-called daughter?"

"Aaa! My brother, who knows? Have you seen the colour of the girl's skin?"
"Hmm! I have. What about her eyes? *Benarau*, they are like cat's eyes-O!"
"And when she throws back her head and laughs, her neck looks like that of a giraffe"

"Ha! What about her white teeth!"

Suitors besieged the Ebikake household when their daughter was barely twelve. She could not help but become conscious of her beauty because young men complimented her all the time. Compliments notwithstanding, the pretty maiden did not look at any of them.

When she attained the age of fourteen, Otou formally asked for her hand in marriage and in keeping with the old promise, the parents happily consented. Younger and wealthier suitors were dumbfounded when news of Otou's betrothal to this great beauty became public. Many the prospective suitors could not come to terms with the fact that the girl of their dreams was to be married to an old hunter of all people!

"Impossible! Unbelievable! He must have used charms or magic! Poor beautiful girl! What a waste!" They lamented.

The marriage process was quickly started and the two families gathered for the ceremony. Hunters and wrestlers decorated their faces with white chalk and danced gaily around the crowded arena. People cheered, clapped and talked excitedly.

In the hustle and bustle, no one noticed that the groom Otou, had quietly slipped out of the house. He jumped into his canoe and paddled furiously and reached his destination in record time. Gun in hand, he walked rapidly into the forest. On reaching the original spot where he saw the old woman and the young girl talking many years ago, he stopped and hid behind a tree. He made sure that he had a clear view of the meeting place. Not long after his arrival, he saw the same old woman approaching the little clearing and at that same moment, he also saw his proposed wife looking extraordinarily beautiful, gliding towards the woman. Both ladies joyfully opened their arms to each other. His heartbeat sounded loud in his ears and he was afraid of being heard and seen. As the happy 'mother' and 'daughter' were about to embrace, Otou fired his gun directly at them.

When the smoke cleared, the place was bare! The two women had simply vanished! As soon as he noticed their disappearance, Otou ran back to where his boat was untied it and paddled with the same speed, using short cuts back to his bride's community. The venue of the marriage ceremony was like a funeral arena. There was commotion everywhere as friends and relatives rushed in and out of the house. Upon enquiry, his mother-in-law told him that her daughter suddenly collapsed and died after being dressed for the marriage ceremony. The whole thing was so mysterious and confusing that several healers and seers had to be invited to intervene.

"*Apoo* Otou!" Gbekemo exclaimed.

"Where have you been? We have been looking everywhere for you! Why did you abandon your wife? Is that how you are going to look after her? Of all the persons we invited to help, it was healer Neminemi who tried the most. Eventually though, he said his best was not enough to revive my daughter and he confirmed that she was truly dead!" she said in a breathless rush.

"Then just now, as you walked in she sneezed and woke up! It's all so mysterious and…"

"Please my dear in-law," Otou said gently,

"Be assured that I never abandoned my wife. At the appropriate time, you will come to understand what I am talking about. Anyway, *oyin nua*! My sweet bride is now very much alive as I can see from the smiles she is beaming at me," he concluded laughing heartily.

It did not take long for the guests and towns people alike to resume festivities, as word of the bride's miraculous recovery was announced from mouth to mouth.

Gbekemo and Ebikake's daughter's marriage ceremony was the most memorable the community had ever seen as the dancing continued until the early hours of the morning.

GLOSSARY

Apoo	–	*Expression of surprise*
Benarau	–	*Sister*
Oyin nua	–	*Thank you, Creator*

THREE MUTURUS

There once lived a happy family of three, in an island called Samalaka. The tall, bearded father of the family Mani worked hard to earn a decent living for his family. Fishing in the high seas was his specialty and he often caught big fish like barracuda and shark. With the income from sale of the fish he built his family a comfortable three-room mud house, plastered with cement and roofed with corrugated iron sheets. His very short, dark-brown-skinned and beautiful wife Mone was a fulltime homemaker though she had a few fish traps for the occasional catch. Mani and Mone's only daughter Muturu was tall like her father. She had long hair, a slightly prominent forehead and luminous dark brown eyes. Her complexion was light and she had the graceful walk of a runway model. The word, 'beauty queen' was used to describe Muturu by everyone in the village where they lived and even by strangers meeting her for the first time.

She was so big for her age that men started asking for her hand in marriage when she was just ten years old! Understandably, Mani was very protective of his daughter.

"Mutumutu! My Mutumutu, come here and listen to what I want to tell you. Keep yourself in your Papa's shadow, you hear! A chick that stays under its mother's wings is always protected." He would counsel.

"Yes, Papa-man! O'wey, Papa-man! My own Papa!" Muturu would sing, smiling and jumping up and down.

"Who can touch me when you are here? Everyone fears my Papa-man because he is the strongest man in the whole wide big world!"

Mani would laugh and clap and clap. For some reason, he was always uncomfortable whenever his daughter was alone. He feared for her safety in the midst of the hawkish suitors any of which could kidnap her.

It was a common practice in those days for a man to kidnap a girl he wanted to marry and later send messengers to her parents. Paradoxically, this was done in the name of love. The kidnapped girl would usually be locked in a room then the prospective husband would sneak in and repeatedly rape her. This would go on until she was subdued and in some cases even impregnated. Some girls were seriously brutalized if they refused to cooperate. The rationale for this practice was that the girl, being shamed and humiliated by the ordeal, would finally or invariable agree to remain with the man as his wife even if she did not like him. Following the girl's acceptance and subsequent approval by her family, the traditional dowry and marriage ceremonies were then performed.

Mani became the envy of his colleagues when he acquired a new fishing boat. He now had more customers than all the other fishermen combined. One day, Mani went out to sea in his newly acquired big boat. Expectations were high that with the favourable tide, he would bring home a sizeable catch. Some of his regular customers made advance payments to ensure that they got the quantity of fish they wanted.

As soon as he started dropping the net, Mani noticed a strong wind. Being an experienced fisherman, he instinctively knew that the waves would show their strength sooner than later. He felt confident that all things considered, he would be able to manage any situation that confronted him. Unfortunately, he underestimated the power of the storm which broke out with ferocity, fanning the waves into angry heights. Mani battled the waves but was easily overpowered. He went down to the bottom of the sea, with pictures of his beloved Muturu, flashing before him.

Fellow fishermen found his bloated body three days after he drowned. Mani's death not only left Muturu vulnerable and inconsolable but also threw the little family into deep mourning. A few good neighbours and relatives rallied round Mone and her daughter until some measure of stability returned to their lives.

By the time Muturu attained the age of fourteen, there were three persistent suitors. Mone encouraged her daughter to marry the cigarette smoking wealthy fisherman with busy eyebrows from Bomadi. Muturu pointed out some flaws in the fisherman's character, which her mother considered inconsequential. She insisted on marrying the slim and tall schoolteacher from Ozobo, though the pot-bellied teary-eyed farmer from Trofani also had a lot to offer. The young lady was confused and indecisive. She did not want to offend her mother and cried silently to her dead father for guidance. In the end, Mone told her daughter to marry all three suitors!

"How can that be Mama? How can you say such a thing!" Muturu exclaimed.

"Never mind my daughter, I know what I am talking about. It will benefit us greatly if you marry the three men." Mone assured but her daughter was not convinced.

"Mama, you know that what you are saying is not possible so stop deceiving yourself. Where have you ever heard that one woman married three men hu-u?"

Mone ignored her daughter and headed for the shrine of the chief priest of Samalaka. He was very happy to see her and confidently told the anxious woman that her problem was already solved.

"It is a small matter my good woman! Just buy a cat, a dog and a goat. Then put your daughter and the three animals into a hut and seal the door. Keep them there for 24 hours and say the following prayer. Oh maker of all things! Oh grantor of all wishes! I want you to give me three Muturus. Grant my request I pray. Thank you! Thank you for answering!"

The chief priest asked her to wait for her miracle, which must happen in twenty-four hours. Moni was very happy and sang all the way to her house. She embraced her daughter excitedly.

"My dear child, I told you not to worry. The chief priest has solved our problem!"

"Really? What did he say? Can I marry the man of my choice and.."

"It is not like that Muturu. First and foremost, a special ceremony has to be performed. Thereafter, you are to be purified in a particular way. It is then and then, that your rightful husband will be revealed to you by the gods. Is that not wonderful my daughter?"

"If you say so Mama! I really like that tall…"

"Stop fretting! I am your mother and I have always looked after you. Since your father's untimely death, I have worked extra hard to take care of you. I know you miss your father very much, especially now that you are getting ready to marry…hmm! I will not disappoint you Muturu. The chief priest is a very experienced seer. Everything will turn out well and you will be happy and your mother too will be happy!"

"Thank you Mama! I know you love me and I am very grateful."

Satisfied that Muturu appreciated her efforts, Moni proceeded to carry out the priest's instructions. Muturu meekly entered the hut with the animals, smiling and talking to them. Moni could hardly sleep that night. She tossed and turned under her mosquito net until dawn.

Exactly twenty-four hours after Muturu and the animals were put inside the hut, three lovely and identical girls emerged from the hut! Mone was in awe of what was before her. The chief priest had once again proved that he was a master diviner! She now had three beautiful daughters instead of one! Three dowries to collect, instead of one! Three sons-in-law, instead of one!

"Oh! Life is good! Life is sweet! Ah, Mani! I wish you could see what I am seeing at this moment! How happy you would have been!" She exclaimed, as tears of joy streamed down her cheeks. She laughed out loud and quickly invited the eager suitors. The girls were carefully hidden, so none of her neighbours knew what was going on. She ensured that the suitors came at different times and she graciously gave out all three girls in marriage to the men. Naturally, each man believed he was marrying the real Muturu.

As time passed, Mone thought it wise to identify her true daughter, the original Muturu. She therefore set out to visit her three sons-in-law. When she got to in-law number one, he complained about his wife's penchant for eating raw plantains. The husband said he could not understand why his wife has bluntly refused to stop the practice.

"I think you should talk to your daughter about it. Surely, plantain tastes better when it is cooked. Even though my wife does not compel me to eat raw food items, I feel it is not natural. Please Mama Mone, do something! I am so glad you are here. I could not talk to my own mother about it because she might read all kinds of meaning...you know what I mean."

"Indeed my son, I know what you mean! I will definitely speak with my daughter and I know she will stop the habit. Please do not worry." Mone assured.

She had planned to spend three nights but left after only one night and travelled to in-law number two's house. Both husband and wife welcomed her with shouts of joy. Mone heaved a sigh of relief, believing that this was her true daughter. The happy mother was about to retire for the night when her son-in-law invited her for a private discussion. Her heart sank.

'Oh please, let this discussion be about the wonderful things my daughter is doing in her matrimonial home. O, let it be that this is my beloved Muturu and not a stranger, with strange cravings,' she prayed silently as she sat down beside her son-in-law.

"Mama Mone, I am so offended by my wife's behaviour. Will you believe me if I tell you that she can't stop licking raw palm oil?"

"Er..r..no! Er..yes! I mean...what I mean is, we all lick raw palm oil occasionally when eating boiled plantain or yam but what you are saying is...." "That, raw palm oil is her regular meal. Mama Mone, it is not good at all! Please advise her before you leave. She even drinks the oil when it is clear and sweet-smelling!"

"I will caution her my son. In fact, I will talk to her before going to bed." She promised. With a heavy heart, Mone went to her daughter's room. Muturu was surprised that her mother had not yet slept after bidding her 'goodnight.'

"Mama, you look worried. Are not feeling well?"

"I am alright my daughter. It's your husband's complaint that is..."

"Oh, Mama! I know! Yes, I like licking palm oil. Frankly Mama, I do not know why. I just cannot help myself when it comes to licking palm oil." At this point, Mone merely patted her daughter's shoulder.

"I understand. Believe me, I do. Goodnight!" She said and left, head bowed.

She did not wait for breakfast the next morning, before leaving her son-in-law's house. Mone's son-in-law genuinely liked her and wanted her to spend more time with the family. She promised to visit them again soon and left.

Her final trip was to son- in-law number three's home. She had barely seated herself when he started complaining bitterly.

"Mama Mone, please do not think I have no respect for you. I know you have just come but I cannot keep hiding the heat burning me up any longer. Your daughter has caused me great embarrassment. How can a human being run after live rats all the time? What is worse is that she eats these rats raw when she catches them! I cannot take it anymore, Mama Mone! She must stop this useless habit immediately or the marriage is over. Can you imagine what members of my family will say if they ever find out? Oh! This is too much! I can't bear it anymore!" The frustrated husband said, biting his fingernails.

"I don't know what to say my son. This is a big blow. My whole world appears to be collapsing and I don't know what to do!" Mone said, weeping uncontrollably.

It has been said times without number that the ear that ignores good advice, will surely follow the head when it is cut off for not listening to wise counsel.

Mone's confusion and grief was great. She could not believe that her beloved daughter was no more!

"O! O! My poor Muturu! Your beautiful soul now taken over by a goat, cat or is it a dog! Eee *oyinma-ooO!*" she wailed.

HUMAN FACED BIRD

My name is Akpai Tolobo. I was born in Koloma, a fairly big town with a mixed population of very poor, fairly well to do and rich people. My family belonged to the very poor group but we were content and envied on one. This predominantly farming and fishing community shared its immediate environment with mangrove swamps. We had only one major thoroughfare situated in front of little shops and residential houses. This 'street' was the hob of village activities. All town gossips began and ended here. Love affairs began here and sometimes ended here. Everyone, rich or poor, relaxed along this street.

The story of my life would have been quite ordinary but for some dramatic events that took place in my family. According to my mother, she had several children before I was born but none survived. Interestingly though, after I was born and survived, two girls and two boys followed me into her womb but only the girls grew to adulthood. I had a normal childhood but was often teased by friends because of my height. I was always the tallest in my classes.

"Tall boy Tolobo, you are equal to a roof-O! Tallingo, Tallingo!" They would tease, pointing at some rooftops.

"You think say any girl go gree marry you soo, Tolobo? I beg, make you 'long' small, small naa!" They would say, laughing.

I usually ignored them because my father had warned me not pick fights with 'those fools.'

I attended the village primary school, after which my parents sent me to live with an uncle in Port Harcourt. My uncle, a skinny tall man with small eyes, was a messenger in the State Government Teachers Institute. His salary was meagre so he could not afford to send me to secondary school since he had children of his own to cater for. I occasionally visited him at work and admired the neatly dressed men who worked as instructors. They usually wore sparking white shirts, adorned with blue ties and well-starched brown shorts. This admiration kindled a burning desire in me that would not go away. I wanted to be like them but what hope did I have of ever achieving my dream, I wondered. I pondered this matter day in and day out.

Exactly one year after coming to live with my uncle, I begged him to at least, enrol me in extramural classes. Three months after I made this request, he located a centre near his house and paid for me to study in the adult beginners section. I was very happy and grateful to him. I studied had and was able to pass six subjects in the General Certificate Examination (GCE). My grades were good: two A's, three B's and one pass. When I showed the result to my uncle, he was extremely happy and gave me a big hug, the very first time he would be showing emotion in this manner.

"O! My good son! Well done! I am proud, very proud of you my boy! O! Good!" He exclaimed over and over.

"Thank you very much, uncle! Without your generosity and care, this day would never have come. I am very grateful, Sir!" I responded, genuflecting deeply.

"With such a result, it will be easy for you to get a job. You can be a clerk or even a teacher." My uncle assured. I knew he was right but something held me back from looking for a job immediately.

By a stroke of fate, one of my young instructors at the extramural centre befriended me during my period of study.

"I am very impressed with your zeal for learning. Continue in this spirit and you will go far in life." he would often remark. I assured him that I had no intention of losing focus, since I consider a good education as a door opener, especially for someone from a poor background. I would often share my hopes and dreams of a bright future with him.

Then one Saturday afternoon when I was busy washing some dirty clothes, my uncle called me in a loud voice.

"Tolobo! Tolobo, you have a visitor!" Surprised, I asked if he meant me. I hardly made friends, preferring to keep to myself so it was inconceivable that anyone would be visiting me.

"Yes, I mean you if your name is Tolobo. Come quickly and attend to your visitor!" He ordered. Murmuring, I rinsed my hands and went to the house.

"What!" I exclaimed, as I saw who the visitor was.

"Don't look so horrified! I have not come to arrest you. This is friendly visit." Said the visitor, laughing.

"Pardon me Sir! I didn't mean to be rude. It's just that I never expected that someone like you will come and…"

"That's alright. Please relax!"

My visitor was none other than the teacher who had befriended me. I had no idea he knew where I lived not to talk of paying me a visit! I was surprised and at same time, worried to see him at our humble three-room Gbundu waterside apartment. The reason I felt these mixed emotions would be better appreciated when I describe our neighbourhood.

The structures here are constructed with plywood and corrugated iron sheets. Apartment walls are so thin that neighbours easily overhear conversations taking place inside each other's bedrooms. Everyone cooked with firewood, so smoke from the open fires entered rooms unchecked. There were no drains and several families shared one pit latrine. When it rains, as it often did faeces, urine and garbage combined to give the pathways a black, slimy, smelly covering. Yes, you guessed right! It rained early that morning! I was therefore quite uncomfortable that such an important visitor had come visiting on such a day and made to apologize. As if reading my mind, he laughed again.

"Do you think I am from the rich part of town eh? I told to calm down my friend. We are all the same." I could only murmur and heave a sigh of relief.

"Oh! I didn't know you are also a mind reader. Thank you for understanding Sir!"

As soon as my uncle was told about the role the man had played in my life, he embraced and thanked him. Drinks were offered but politely refused.

With everyone now relaxed, he told me why he had come. A great opportunity had been offered to him. He was leaving for the United States of America (USA) to study, not because his family was wealthy but because he had been offered a scholarship. I begged him to give me details of the scholarship scheme and how I could also apply. My friend did more than just give me details. He came with an application form and assisted me to fill it out before leaving for the United States. Six months later, I wrote the relevant examinations and was awarded a full overseas scholarship! My happiness, as you can imagine was boundless. I had jumped from dreamland into the realm of reality! My scores afforded me the choice of studying in Europe, Canada or United States of America. I naturally chose the United States because my former teacher was studying there. Better be where you know at least one person, I reasoned.

I sent word to my parents in Koloma about my good fortune and even before the excitement had died down, I was inside an aeroplane, flying high in the sky! Several emotions crowded my being as I sat comfortably in the aircraft. Who would have thought that a gangly six-foot-six boy like me from remote Koloma, would one day be awarded a scholarship to study outside my country? I pinched my lap and smiled.

'You are on a plane o'l boy! You are actually going to *pena-ebe*! The ancestors are alive! They are working! Tolobo, no one can wake you up from this dream because it is real and you are wide awake!'

When the plane touched down in the United States, New York City to be precise, I was awed by the glitter and buzz of everything. Who wouldn't? White faces and more white faces everywhere! I was culture shocked no doubt but no one looking at me would have guessed it. As directed, I took a train to my University where I met a lot of new students like me. It was so exciting to see 'civilization' in action! The international students' affairs officer of the University helped me a lot and I settled down quickly.

Being conscious of where I was coming from, I studied hard. There were distractions no doubt, particularly the breathtakingly beautiful girls. O, how dazzling and absolutely tempting they looked but I did my best not to lose focus. I wrote home regularly, telling my parents everything about my life in the white man's land. They felt I was exaggerating when describing the tall buildings called 'skyscrapers,' the fast-moving trains, the 'fast foods', the twenty-four hour lights and many more.

My mother especially thought I could send her money since I appeared to have settled down fairly quickly. I explained that, that would happen after I had graduated and secured a well-paying job. It was difficult for her to understand how a son in America could not send even a few dollars! After all, America they were told, was a land flowing with milk and honey. Could the stories of dollars everywhere be false, she would ask.

In my quiet moments, I would often reflect on my uncle's wise words. Of particular interest to me was the one about a child leaving home without his parent's consent. He noted that such a child should be careful of actions that would bring or return evil report. In my own case, I left home with the consent of my parents but I was still very careful of who I interacted with. Reports abounded of young men, who followed the glitter and got themselves into big trouble. Many were unable to graduate because they joined criminal gangs or became drug addicts. Deportations of such persons were not as uncommon as people thought.

After five years of dedicated study, I was awarded a Bachelor of Science degree in Criminology and a Masters degree in advanced Mind Technology. I was among the best five graduating students so I was confident that getting a good job would be easy.

I applied to many important organizations but could not secure a job and this was a big surprise to friends who knew the quality of my degrees. This was the situation until my friend Endiowei, introduced me to one Mr Funky Jack. A fat, jovial and compassionate man with dusty red hair. He offered me a job that was not too interesting. This notwithstanding, I gladly took it because I needed to take care of myself now that the scholarship money was no more. It was my first fulltime employment, two years after graduation.

From the moment I started work with Funky Jack, I knew my life would change for the better. The man inspired me. He was philosophical and funny but firm. Many called him a liberal democrat who minded his own business. There was an employee retirement scheme for individuals who had worked for at least two years but he told me to avail myself if I so desired. It sounded good and generous to me so I immediately signed up. With the requisite deductions being regularly made, I felt secure in the job.

One bright summer morning shortly after I resumed work, Funky Jack called me to his office and informed me that I would be having a visitor from home soon. Before I could ask who, he calmly told me that the visitor was none other than my mother. I laughed out loud!

"You must be joking! You are joking, right Funky?" I asked.

"Nope! I am not joking, my man!" He replied.

"But this is crazy, man! There is no way in heaven my mother could afford a trip to the U.S. It is impossible! You know Funky, my mother even refused to visit Port Harcourt, a city that's in Nigeria and..." Funky Jack held up his right hand to stop me. He looked at me steadily.

"We'll see! Tolobo my boy, you go about your job now. Your ma will come whether you believe it or not!"

At this point, I was no longer laughing. Everyone knew how generous the boss was. Could it be that he had decided to foot the bill for such a trip as a reward for my dedicated service to the company, I wondered. He must really love me very much and not just because of my dedication to duty, to incur such expenses for my sake I also reasoned. I could not ask him directly of course but assumed that this must be the case, so adopted a wait and see attitude.

Two days after my conversation with Funky Jack, two beautiful white ladies paid me a visit after work when I was about to have dinner. As I sought to know their mission, one of them started scolding me for not taking care of my parents back home.

"Who are you and what do you know about my background? Are you agents of the secret service or what?" I asked the women, who now tried to placate me by smiling broadly. I felt that the strangers didn't have the right to meddle in my affairs and told them to leave but they pleaded that I take them to my boss, Funky Jack. They claimed to have an important business to transact with him. I phoned Funky and he said it was okay, so I took them to his house.

"Hi Ladies! What can I do for you?" He asked as soon they sat down. They looked at each other before the short one with blood red hair and blue eyes started speaking.

"Well Mr Jack, we think Tolobo is an irresponsible man. How can he spend close to seven years in America and not send even a few dollars home to his family?"

Funky smiled faintly and gazed steadily at the women. Before I realized what was happening, one of them had slipped out of the living room. Without removing his gaze from the other one, Funky told me that she was the visitor he mentioned a few days earlier. I was speechless!

"Yes!" Everyone was in full agreement because they knew that there was no other choice. No other cause of action was available for the community. Their enemies must be destroyed. The deliberations ended by midnight and members of council dispersed to make final preparations.

When King Hata returned to his sitting room, with its walls of lavishly decorated leopard, zebra and lion skins, he could not relax. Though it was late, sleep eluded him and before long, he heard the throaty crow a cock.

"Koko..roo..koo! Kooko..roo..koo!" It crowed delightedly, announcing the approach of yet, another day. Nature's cycles wait for no one and like it or not, dawn pushes night aside at precisely the right moment in time. Hata sighed and hissed, for perhaps, the ten thousandth time! This particular day dawned with robust brightness. The birds sang with the melodiousness of a heavenly choir but the king of Lagai kingdom noticed none of these beautiful occurrences.

It was around eleven in the morning when his beloved daughter, the crown princess Nikpi, joyfully ran to her father for the customary hug but he asked her to leave. The princess was surprised. He had never treated her like this before, in all her fourteen years on earth. She instinctively knew that the kingdom was in danger. Wise beyond her years, Nikpi made discreet enquiries and discovered that war with their neighbours was imminent. In the days following, King Hata called Nikpi to his sitting room six times in six days, without his customary petting or hugging. He was always distracted. However, when he summoned her for the seventh time, Nikpi, realizing that something very grave must be happening to her father talked to him tenderly. She sat at his feet and gently massaged his toes one by one.

"Papa, I know that Lagai will win the war. You are a great king. You always win!" She told him confidently.

"My dear child, my princess you are right, you are always right!" He replied, stroking her soft hair, cut short and adorned with pink coral beads.

"If I am right Papa, why have you been sad these past six days? Is it the commanders? Are they not...."

"O no! My princess, it is not what you think."

"Then what is it father please tell me what the problem is." She pleaded.

Unable to look at his daughter and fighting to overcome the temporary weakness that threatened to overwhelm him, Hata took a deep breath and sighed then stood up. He paced up and down for several seconds before finally drumming up enough courage to face his daughter. Enfolding her in a fierce embrace he began.

"You my wise and beautiful Nikpi are my child of destiny. Your father loves you beyond what words can say. It is no surprise to me that you feel my pain and know how troubled I have been. My dearest child, the oracle has decreed that a virgin must be sacrificed before we can be victorious in the impending war. Hmm! Err..hmm! That virgin my beloved daughter is you!" He whispered, fighting back tears.

"I thought as much my father when you sent for me so many times without saying anything. So unlike you!" Nipki murmured.

She stood up, biting her nails and walked to the end of the room and back, head bowed. Then with a determined shake of her head and amazing calmness, told her father that community survival must take priority over everything else.

"I will obey. I accept the oracle's verdict but you must allow me six days of feasting and playing with my friends. They will miss me much and I will miss them too."

"Oh beloved of my heart and soul, your wish is granted!" Her father responded, almost choking on his words.

With a heart burdened by sorrow, king Hata reconvened the war council. There were no smiles and everyone was sad, as the King told them what had to be done. He instructed that the main river, through which the enemy would come, was to be poisoned at its source. He also ordered that the seven slave girls who had been chosen to be used as underlay for the princess be ritually prepared according the customs of the land. It was fitting and proper that they be cleansed since princess Nikpi was to be buried alive on top of them. The royal princess had to be accorded the highest respect for the noble role she had agreed to play on behalf of the entire Lagai kingdom. Accordingly, all the chiefs went in solemn procession to her apartment and paid her the traditional homage due a princess of such high quality. Nikpi acknowledged their greetings with smiles and a wave of her fan, made of eagle feathers and tiny crystals. The chiefs had expected her to wear a mournful look but were quite amazed by her calm and bright countenance. Their respect for the young princess increased and they were so moved that a number of them discreetly wiped their faces to hide the tears they could not help shedding.

On the day she was to be sacrificed, Nikpi came out to the public square walking majestically. Her attire of expensive white velvet wrapper sparkled in the early morning sun. Rare pink and red coral beads were used to decorate her hair, neck, wrists and ankles. She held her eagle feathers fan as well as a white ox tail whisk, a decorated symbol of office. Forty young girls, faces painted with red chalk and wearing short white dresses, led her through the town as citizens cheered. She stood heads and shoulders above them all. The girls sang songs praising Nikpi for her heroism. As the procession reached the graveside, Nikpi solemnly raised her hands skywards eyes closed. The high priest poured libations, followed by intense incantations. The spectators looked on in awe as they noticed several white doves flying close to Nikpi, as if bidding her farewell. A special drumbeat sounded in the distance as she was lifted by two warriors clad in red gowns and gently lowered into the grave. The seven slave girls inside the grave were still, as if already dead when the princess was placed on top of them. All trading in Lagai was suspended for one day, as a mark of respect and honour for Nikpi.

Following the sacrifice of Nikpi, the Lagai went into battle with the Nukuys. Interestingly, the enemy appeared to have been defeated even before arms were used. The reason for this was simple. Many of their warriors perished at the river after drinking its poisoned waters. One of the enduring legacies of the Lagai-Nukuy war is the 'loss' of otherwise valuable river fish. It is said that fish caught in the Lagai River refuses to cook, no matter how long it is boiled! Even when thrown into a pot of boiling water, fish from this river remains very much alive!

The Lagai people did not forget the noble role princess Nikpi played to ensure the survival of their kingdom. Consequently, a befitting monument has been constructed at the site of her sacrificial burial and the place has remained a tourist attraction ever since.

YAYA'S CHILD

Kerebi was a boisterous man. Fat, with a double chin and pregnant-looking belly, he was loved by many because of his easy-going manner and booming laughter. He had a good source of income, selling food items and bales of wrappers. Kerebi managed his business well and achieved his dream of building a three-bedroom house by the time he was just twenty-five years old. His next plan was to settle down properly by getting married. He was not interested in marrying just any woman but the most beautiful one in the entire clan.

"You are fooling yourself!" his friend Ebikare told him, laughing.

"Take a good look at yourself, my man. Money is not everything-O! Girls like men who are handsome and..."

"Now, who is fooling himself? So..o.o! You think girls of nowadays care about long nose, white teeth and all the other assets that combine to make a man handsome, ehh? My friend, you are a dreamer of the highest order. Just wait and see!"

"Ha, Kerebi! I can tell you categorically that I Ebikare, the Mr. Handsome of the clan, will have collected all the beauty queens before you get to their doors!" he boasted, showing off his abs before doing a Michael Jackson moon walk.

"Ha! Ha! Ha! I can't wait to see your face when I arrive home with my bride, the most beautiful girl in the clan. *Na dat time you go know say moni get power pass fine face."* Kerebi told his friend, beating his chest for emphasis.

The two friends chatted for a while longer, slapping each other's backs.

Barely one year after the above conversation took place, Kerebi got married to young and beautiful Yaya, a well-known dancing champion. Ebikare was on hand to welcome his friend's bride. As soon as it was convenient to do so he pulled his friend to a corner.

"Congratulations O'l boy but what happen? I thought you said…"

"Well, I agree that she is not a beauty queen but her character is a hundred times more…"

"That is not the point. You beat your chest and boasted that the most beautiful girl in the clan will be your wife. *Make you no dey beat chest anyhow abeg! I for fine you well, well if no bi say you bi my correct guy…"*

"Thank you but the promise *never die-O! I still marry…"*

"Abeg stop dat kain talk!" Ebikare told his friend, laughing.

The young couple settled down to married life and Yaya proved to be a big asset. She was shrewd and industrious. Kerebi was happy with his wife but was worried that there was no pregnancy in sight, one whole year after their marriage. Yaya was very perceptive and noticed that her husband was now fond of making references to friends or relatives whose wives had given birth in such and such village or town.

"Don't worry my husband, I will go to Amigidi for thorough massage. She has the reputation of detecting even unsuspected gynaecological troubles and will surely find out why I have not being able to conceive…"

"Look, I am not accusing you of bareness or…"

"O my husband! I did not say you are accusing me of anything. It is the responsibility of a young wife to give her husband children and that is what I want to do."

"In that case, I encourage you to see the woman as soon as possible. Just let me how much you will need." He said, smiling broadly.

Yaya visited Amigidi that very evening for preliminary consultations. After just a few minutes of cursory examination, the famous masseur nodded.

"You will conceive when the next moon shows its smiling face. Come back tomorrow morning before sunrise. There is nothing seriously wrong with your womb." Amigidi assured.

The anxious young wife ran home, relieved that she was not barren after all. Kerebi too was very happy when he learnt that his wife was quite fertile. The treatment commenced immediately and as predicted, Yaya became pregnant the next month. Though the pregnancy was a difficult one, the expectant mother remained cheerful. She and her husband looked forward to the birth of their first child with excitement. When the child was eventually born, Yaya was happy that it was a girl. A female first born signified prosperity and an easy life for the parents so she could not have wished for anything better. Kerebi on the other hand could not be said to be overjoyed. Yes, he knew that the general belief was that if your firstborn was female life would treat you better but still, it would have been nice to have a son to prove one's prowess. He wondered if this was a sign that his first wife did not have male eggs in her biological system. He made up his mind then and there to marry a second wife. There was no need to take chances on matters as crucial as the production of male children to carry on the family name and lineage.

One year after the birth of Yaya's child, Kerebi informed his wife that he had decided to marry a second wife. Yaya knew that there was nothing she could do about her husband's decision.

"When are you bringing her home?" She asked.

"The next market day. Her name is Boemi. I am sure you will like her. She is very respectful and …"

"It is alright my husband. We shall welcome her when she comes."

Boemi's arrival was without fanfare. Yaya welcomed the new member of the family formally with an embrace and took her to the apartment she was to occupy. Kerebi invited his wives for a brief meeting to acquaint them with the new house rules and sleeping formula. Each wife was expected to sleep with him for two weeks at a time during which time, she would also be responsible for preparing his meals.

Yaya the first wife, started experiencing body pains about six months after her husband married Boemi. The pains became so severe that she became house bound for months before recovering a little. Yaya lost her ability to trade actively so Kerebi asked Boemi to take over her shop. Kerebi had expected his second wife to get pregnant quickly but that was not the case. Boemi went from healer to healer but conception eluded her. Kerebi was tempted to marry a third wife since Yaya's chronic illness made it difficult for her to conceive. Then, three years after he paid the full bride price and made her a wife, Boemi became pregnant. The happy husband and wife heaved a sigh of relief.

"It is going to be a boy!" Boemi predicted.

"I will buy you the most expensive wrapper in the market for you if it is a boy as you say. It's high time I rub shoulders with Ebikare, whose wife has given birth to two boys already."

"I thought you said they've been married for..."

"Only three years!" He exclaimed.

"Throw your worries away my husband. Mothers have a way of knowing these things." She said confidently, playfully poking her husband's stomach. Kerebi made sure Boemi enjoyed all the comfort a woman in her condition deserved. He bought her little presents every market day. When the ninth month came and there was no sign of labour pains, Kerebi panicked. He ran to Amigidi their family 'doctor.' She assured him that there was nothing to worry about.

"The child has not finished gathering the properties to be used on this side. There are also some errands the parents on the other side want completed. These are normal things Kerebi. There's no cause for alarm and..."

"I hope the child is a boy?" He asked.

"Hmm! I am not at liberty to reveal. The spirits must be obeyed. Be patient my son. You will know soon enough."

With these words of assurance still ringing in his ears, Kerebi went to his friend Ebikare's house.

"Hey Keres, what's up? You are smiling and that means one thing. Huge profits from..."

"Haa! Why are you talking as if my whole life revolves around money and..."

"Women!" Ebikare said, laughing loudly.

"Very funny indeed! On a serious note though I just wanted to tell you the outcome of my visit to Amigidi."

"Oo! What did you go to her for? Hope your wife is..."

"My wife is fine but I have been so worried. The child's time to be delivered is overdue and that's why I went to Amigidi for consultations."

"What did she say?"

"She assured that the child will be born soon but refused to tell me the gender. No matter how much I pleaded she was adamant, claiming that the spirits forbade such disclosures. Ebisco, I am really hoping for a boy. I mean, look at you and your sons! People seem to respect you more if you have sons because they can fight for you when…"

"I know how you feel my man Keres but these things are beyond us. Nobody can claim to be responsible for giving birth to a particular gender. We must accept what is divinely provided."

"You are right of course. When did you become so calm and wise?" He asked, looking at his friend with respect.

Boemi's long awaited child came into the world on a wet and windy night, ten months after she was conceived. The labour was long and difficult but Amigidi was able manage the situation with the help of one assistant. Kerebi remained in his room, drinking freshly brewed gin. By the time the midwife's assistant informed him of his wife's successful delivery of a bouncing baby girl, he was heavily drunk.

"Kerebi, did you hear what I just told you?" The woman asked.

"I said you are the father of a beautiful baby girl!" The effect of the gin appeared to have automatically cleared from his brain as he jumped up and screamed.

"Ohh! A girl you say? She delivered a girl and not a boy? What have I done to offend the gods that has caused them to punish me like this? Oo *akpo-agh!*" He exclaimed over and over. Mellowed by the gin, his lamentations were accompanied by copious crying. He did not bother to call on his wife but went straight to bed. The next day dawned with an early morning sun. It took longer than usual for Kerebi to get out of bed. His eye were red and swollen so he went to the river for a long swim before asking for his breakfast. He reflected on the events of the previous evening and could not help but recall the words of his friend, Ebikare. By late afternoon, he had composed himself well enough to visit his wife and baby.

"I know how deeply disappointed you are, my husband. I really wanted the child to be a boy. Please forgive me. It is not…"

"Please my wife, it is not your fault. I have to be honest and tell that I am disappointed but who has the power to dictate to the Creator of all beings, anh? Let us be grateful you and our lovely daughter are well."

"Oh, thank you for understanding. You are a good husband and I am sure the next child will be a boy. I want to make you happy and I know giving you a boy will bring great joy."

There were tears in their eyes as they embraced. Kerebi firmly believed that Boemi was capable of giving him male children and looked forward to another pregnancy in the not too distant future. They joked about whose features the child had.

Life quickly returned to normal for the Kerebi household after all the anxiety of the previous few weeks. Yaya's health was still a source of concern and her husband was compelled to visit her paternal family to solicit support for further treatment. In spite all the various treatment centres visited and assurances received, Yaya could not overcome her illness and joined her ancestors, just before her daughter's tenth birthday. Her little girl was inconsolable. She cried every day and refused to go out of the house. The depth of her grief surprised Kerebi, who did everything in his power to console her. What he didn't release was the level of maturity the child had attained in the process of looking after her sick mother. Though so young, the child became a mother of sorts. Yaya's child gradually stabilized and father and daughter became very close.

Boemi, the second wife was not too fond of her late mate's child and ensured that a lot of household chores were assigned to her. Though a number of cousins, nieces and nephews lived with the Kerebi family as was typical in many African households, Boemi preferred to allow Yaya's child do most of the housework.

One rainy day, Yaya's little girl was sent to wash a basket-full of aluminium plates at the community stream. While rinsing the plates, one got lost but Yaya's child did not know. The loss did not however escape her stepmother's observant notice. She was promptly sent back to the stream to look for the missing plate. Crying bitterly and completely wet, she slowly walked back to the stream. Fortunately, she saw the plate floating about twenty feet from shore. Relieved, she quickly jumped into the stream and swam to retrieve it. As soon as she touched the plate, it disappeared. At the same time, she found herself in a beautiful compound underwater! The owner of the premises, a beautiful old lady with long black hair and shining cream coloured skin came out to meet her.

"What do you want little girl? Why are you in my compound?" Shaking with fear, Yaya's child spoke in a halting whisper.

"*Okoide okosu-ere*! I was sent by my stepmother to wash plates and one got lost. She asked me to go back to the stream and find it. I found the plate but it disappeared. Next thing I knew, I found myself here in your compound. Please do not...."

"That is alright my child. Hush! There is no need to cry. I will help you." The woman told her in a gentle voice.

"Will you recognize the plate if you see it?"

"Yes!" She replied, nodding nervously.

The woman brought out a number of plates and Yaya's child immediately identified and collected her own. The old woman further told the little girl to go behind a particular hut and take any box of her choice.

Now relaxed, she looked around the place curiously and noted that there were five houses and three huts, all roofed with straw. All the buildings were hand-painted with ashes. The external walls had red, blue and black drawings of different types of fish. The whole area was spotlessly clean. When she got to the back of the hut, she heard loud singing. Surprisingly, it came from inside the neatly arranged boxes!

The big ones sang, "*boekire kon, bo ekire kon!*" while the small ones chorused, "*kon-agh kpo brasin, kon-agh kpo brasin!*"

As the singing continued, she noticed that the biggest boxes sang the loudest. Not impressed, she picked a small one after which the old woman gave her a gentle push. Before she knew what was happening, Yaya's child found herself at the bank of the river. She happily ran home with the plate and box. After giving her stepmother the plate, she called her father into a side room and showed him the box.

"How did you come by this? Have I not warned you against taking things that do not belong to you?" he scolded.

Yaya's child explained how she got it. Father and daughter opened the box and were thoroughly taken aback by the contents. The little box contained money, gold, coral beads, silk cloth, shoes and earrings and decorative combs! Their shouts of joy attracted other members of the family who rushed into the room. They opened their mouths in wonder and could not believe their eyes!

Stepmother Boemi became so envious that she decided to send her own daughter to the same river to wash plates as well. The girl was instructed to deliberately lose one plate! Boemi's daughter did as she was told and eventually found herself in the underwater compound. She answered all questions put to her, just like her half sister and was asked to pick out the missing plate. When faced with the singing boxes, she decided to collect one of the biggest. On arrival home, she called her mother into their main bedroom and locked the door before opening the big box. As they did so, two deadly snakes sprang out and bit them to death. Their screams attracted family members who were horrified by what they saw.

GLOSSARY

Akpo-agh	-	*O, life!*
Boekirekon, kon-agh	-	
kpo brasin	-	*Come and take me, leave me if you like.*
Okoide okosu-ere	-	*I kneel to greet you, old woman.*

EBIOWEI

A man called Demene had three sons whom he loved very much. They carried out their daily activities of fishing and farming diligently. The Demenes were peace loving and lived in harmony with their neighbours. Demene's wife Akwa, died suddenly of an unknown ailment when her last child was just four years old. Everyone in the family expected the grief-stricken husband to overcome his loss after some months of mourning and remarry. Demene refused to have anything to do with women, years after the death of his wife. His kinsmen were worried and advised him to marry a suitable woman at least, for the sake of his children. Even his children joined in appealing to their father but he was not interested. When everyone realised that the man would never remarry, they left him alone even as people continued to speculate that he could be impotent. He kept to himself most times. As time went on, his children noticed that he was fond of going into the forest by himself for long periods. This was the situation when he called them together one day and announced that his time on earth was coming to an end.

"Ah! Papa, how can you say such a thing when you are not sick? I can understand if…"

"You are right my son. I understand why you are surprised but the fact still remains that the time for me to join my beloved wife is imminent." He told his first son. The other two looked at each other and said nothing so their father continued.

"My children, I have decided to make a 'living will' so that you can all continue to live in peace. The ancestors are already waiting at the waterside.

My waist begs to be rested all the time. I want the three of you to share my few properties equally. Please do not go against my decision. All my worldly possessions must be shared equally as I said before. None must have more than the other. That is my wish and you will all live better than I did, if you follow my instructions." Demene said, looking into their eyes intently.

What he asked them to share consisted of a mud house, a fowl, a small farmland and a goat. About a month after making this living will, Demene went to sleep one night with a smile on his face and did not wake up the next day. His youngest son was the first person to see his father's body and he could not really believe that the promised exist had come. The older brothers and other family members were quickly informed. Demene was given a dignified burial and was mourned by those who loved him.

After the observance of a three-day mandatory post burial set of activities, the eldest son invited his brothers for a meeting to share their father's properties. It was customary to involve members of the extended family so they were dully invited to witness the sharing.

"In spite of what our father said, it is my right as your elder brother to have the lion's share of his properties therefore, I am taking the farmland and the house." Some members of the extended family agreed with him, arguing that it was unjust and goes against tradition to deprive the firstborn son of the lion's share.

"Well, as the second son, I am entitled to the goat," said brother number two.

Ebiowei the last-born was left with only the fowl, which he reluctantly took.

His elder brother did very well with his farm. The house too was well utilized. He partitioned it and rented out several rooms. In less than two years, he had become rich.

The second brother with the goat, also did well. He entered into a partnership with a herdsman and their business grew. This brother too became a prosperous man three years after his father's death. Late Demene's prediction appeared to have come true in the lives of his first two sons but surely, the last son too must have been included in this vision of prosperity? How is it then that he was not able to rise above his former status?

As much as he tried, Ebiowei made little progress. He was miserable because he just did not know what to do with his fowl that could yield some reasonable income. After years of fruitless struggle, he decided to tend a parcel of farmland belonging to his late mother. He planted yams, cassava, cocoyams and corn. During the first harvest, his yams did well and he stored them neatly in a barn at the back of his house.

While working in his farm one day, a woman came to him asking for a tuber of yam.

"Please give me some yam to eat, I am very hungry," she begged and he readily agreed.

As time went on, his fowl started laying eggs. Annoyingly, a snake broke the eggs, sucked the yolks and was slithering away when Ebiowei brought out his gun to shoot it.

"O please, don't shoot me! I sucked the yolks because I was hungry. Spare my life Ebiowei!" It pleaded. Ebiowei reluctantly put down his gun and allowed the snake go. Since a few of the eggs had hatched, he reasoned that in a few months time his fowls would have increased. However, this was not to be as an eagle swooped on the chicks and ate them! Ebiowei was really furious and again brought out his gun to shoot the offending predator.

"Please have mercy! I was very hungry and had nowhere else to go. Pity me and spare my life!" It cried.

The compassionate Ebiowei forgave the eagle and let it go. As this was going on the woman who had earlier asked for yam came back, crying in distress and requested for more yams. Being soft hearted, Ebiowei agreed to assist her once more. The woman thanked him and departed but returned shortly thereafter with her husband who accused Ebiowei of raping his wife! He attacked Ebiowei with sticks and reported him to the local vigilante, who summarily tried and locked him up in the community cell. The thoroughly confused Ebiowei could not believe what just happened to him!

"What is the meaning of this? I thought I was helping a person in need! No wonder Pere-owei used to tell me that when you are courteous to a man you are eating with, the ingredients in the soup would think you are afraid of them!" He sighed.

"Your parables do not impress me, you rapist! Men like you must not be spared. You are lucky I did not cut off your hands!" The angry husband told Ebiowei.

While in detention, the snake he spared visited him.

"My dear Ebiowei, the princess of ATANGBALA will be bitten by me tomorrow." It said.

"I will give you a leaf which is the antidote that will revive her. I have decided to do you this favour because you spared my life."

"Oh, really! That's very nice of you. Many would not have remembered so I thank you for coming to my aid."

Ebiowei waited in anticipation. He didn't have long to wait. News came the very next day that the king's daughter had died of snakebite. Atangbala was thrown into mourning. Ebiowei quickly sent word to the community elders that he had the capacity to revive the princess. The chiefs and advisers were not impressed. If such a miracle worker existed in the Kingdom, they would have heard about him. They did not want to give false hope to a father already in deep mourning.

"What if this unknown healer turns out to be genuine? Let us not claim to be wiser than the king. He must be informed and let him decide how best to treat the man." The chief adviser told them.

They looked at each other and nodded in agreement thereafter, the king was duly informed.

"What did you say? There is someone claiming to have the ability to bring my precious daughter back to life? I do not care if he is an imposter, a dreamer or a mad man! He must be given the opportunity to prove or disprove his claim. Send for him at once!" He ordered.

Ebiowei was taken before the king without delay.

"O healer! I will offer you half of the kingdom and the princess's hand in marriage, if you can bring her back to life as you claim." The king proclaimed.

"I will do my best O great King! If you can take me to the room where the princess is, I will be glad to commence treatment immediately. Let not your mind be troubled further, mighty King of Atangbala. I give you my word that the princess will smile and dance for her father before the sun stands in the middle of the sky, this very day." He promised, smiling.

"Chief adviser, take him to the door of the princess's chamber and tell her mother that it is alright for the stranger to see the princess." The king instructed.

Ebiowei ignored the women and knelt by the princess's bed, then proceeded to administer the antidote. The room was quiet as everyone literally heard their breath. Ebiowei recited some incantations, shook his head several times and whispered. He appeared to be communicating with an invisible entity. After a few minutes the princess's mother noticed beads of sweat on the healer's forehead and her heart sank. She deliberately turned her back to prevent people from noticing the tears of disappointment that had gathered in her eyes. Shortly thereafter, the princess's eyelids gradually opened as Ebiowei spoke gently into her right ear. She opened her eyes wide and smiled!

"My queen behold, your daughter!" Ebiowei said to the princess's mother who shouted for joy. All the screaming, shouting and laughing, surprised the princess because she did not know that she was actually dead but later brought back to life.

The extremely happy king kept his promise and Ebiowei not only became a prince but also a very wealthy and powerful man. Pa Demene saw into the future after all!

LIFE'S TURNS

Brasoro, the town crier of Ogbouba was a boisterous man and interacted well with both the young and old in the town.

"Well, you do not have to shout all the time because you are a town crier. The gong is there to make all the noise when you beat it or do you want to tell me that you..."

"Eee! Am I the one you are insulting like a small child? I do not blame you at all Obomo! When a twenty-year old begins to play moon light games with ten-year olds, he should not expect adult conversation."

"Aaa Brasoro, it is not like that. How can I insult you? It's just that you talk so loudly and it affects my ears. Please do not be offended. You are my favourite brother-in-law and I do not want my sister to think that I do not respect her husband."

"Have no fear. This conversation will not get to the ears of my beloved Egbeide."

Brasoro was married to two women. His first wife Egbeide, bore him three daughters, while Youmu the second wife, had only one daughter, Emi. Youmu was a very hardworking woman. She went to her farm one day and was in the process of felling a tree when a branch fell on her head. The injuries she sustained led to her death. She was just twenty years old and her death marked a sad turn in the life of her daughter, Emi.

Even though there were several cousins in the Brasoro household, the stepmother Egbeide, preferred sending Emi to do most household chores. From cooking to washing to sweeping, Emi did all. In spite this, she was usually scolded and beaten for minor offenses or unavoidable delays. Brasoro was not happy that Emi was the only one he always saw doing the housework. He drew his wife's attention to this anomaly several times.

"Egbeide, you better stop this wicked behaviour. How can you allow one child alone do all the work in the house? Are your daughters cripples? Do you think teaching them to be lazy is love?" He would scold.

"*A-boo*! Brasoro! So my daughters are now lazy girls eh? Yes! I know! Emi is your favourite daughter! The rest of us will soon leave this house for the two of you. Nonsense!" Egbeide would hiss.

Egbeide forbade her daughters from 'soiling' their hands with housework. There were however brief periods of relief for Emi. The youngest of her half-sisters Torke-ere, was not happy with the situation and occasionally helped out, though secretly. Emi's predicament confirmed the universally held view that no child enjoys staying with her stepmother.

Ebgeide's intolerance and maltreatment of her stepdaughter reached a climax when the girl was driven away from home. Egbeide had instructed Emi to cook two pots of soup for her half sisters and when it was time to eat the food, the girls complained that the soup was sour. Their mother became very angry and started screaming.

"You evil girl! You want to kill my daughters so that you will become the only child in this family. Get out of this house you witch! I will show you what wickedness is if you ever come back!" She shouted, beating Emi with a stick.

With tears streaming down her face, Emi wandered from place to place. The only shelter available was an abandoned building, where she slept for a week before help came her way. Her late mother's cousin had heard about the girl's troubles from a friend. Worried, she sent some young girls to look for her. When Emi was eventually found and taken to her mother's cousin, the woman could not control her tears. There were mosquito bite marks all over the girl's body and her feet were covered with blisters.

"You will never go back to your father's house my child. Never! How could your father allow that witch treat you like a slave! May the spirit of my cousin visit and haunt them both!" She swore.

One year after this incident, Egbeide's first daughter got married. The young husband was a traditional man and expected his wife to cook for him. The bride was gripped by anxiety since she did not know how to cook. She had to think fast! After much thought, the young bride came up with a grand plan. Things would be arranged in such a way that her husband would always be out of the house when it was time to cook. Her mother would then come in and cook several pots of assorted meals.

Meanwhile, Emi's guardian who had recently married a wealthy trader threw a big party to celebrate the birth of their first son. Important dignitaries from many communities were invited and Emi cooked the main dishes. All who ate the food commented on how delicious the meals tasted. The hostess casually mentioned to a few close friends that the food was cooked by her protégée. Unknown to her, a wealthy young businessman overheard the conversation. He later approached the hostess and congratulated her on the overall success of the party emphasizing how much he enjoyed the meal.

"I overheard you telling your friend that the tasty food we just ate was cooked by a young lady. I hope you will not be offended if I ask you to introduce me to the her?" He asked politely.

"O! I am glad you enjoyed the food, chief…."

"Ah, forgive me for not introducing myself madam. My name is Bibowei Temezigha."

"Alright Bibowei, I will be happy to arrange a meeting between you and my niece. She will be flattered that many people loved her tasty meals, including a handsome man like you." She told him, smiling broadly.

Emi's guardian kept her word and introduced Bibowei to Emi before the party ended. The two appeared to like each other and discussed at length before Bibowei left.

Less than a year after the above conversation took place, Emi became Mrs Temezigha. The marriage between Emi and Bibowei was attended by friends and family from far and near. Many described it as the most glamorous marriage the town had ever seen. Emi was happy because her husband loved her very much. He pampered her and provided whatever she desired. The maltreatment suffered at the hands of her stepmother became a distant memory.

Life was good for Emi but the same could be not said of her elder sister. She was finding things a bit difficult and the marriage was not turning out the way she anticipated. Her husband's dissatisfaction about most things she did made her cry often. She felt unappreciated and unloved.

"O my husband, why are you never impressed with whatever I do in this house?" She asked.

"Well, I think you just don't have the right training to be a good housewife. You do not even know how to talk to someone. In short, you lack good manners!"

"Please, I am ready to learn. Do not turn away from me."

"That's fine. You know I love you and I want us live in harmony." He said, enfolding her in his arms. Things appeared to improve afterwards but unknown to the young madam, her husband had become increasingly uncomfortable with his wife's decision to always have him out of the house before preparing meals. He therefore, decided to set a trap for her. On a particular morning when he noticed that his wife was unhappy, he told her that he had to embark on an emergency trip.

"This is a very important business trip and I am hoping to make a lot of money. I should be back in two weeks. I am going to buy a velvet wrapper for you from the city. The type you've been eyeing since we got married."

"O, my loving husband! Thank you very much! Please buy the red one and a pair of shoes to match-o!" She said, giving him a bid hug.

Two hours after the relieved wife waved her husband goodbye, he sneaked back into the compound. The yam barn situated behind the main building was the perfect hiding place. He didn't have long to wait before he saw his mother-in-law entering the house with a bag full of foodstuff. Though he was surprised to see her, he waited for another hour before rushing into the house. His unexpected appearance exposed his wife's deceit as he saw his mother-in-law busy cooking in the kitchen. Feeling tricked, he asked his mother-in-law to leave immediately.

"Please, take your lazy daughter with you as well. This marriage is over! Do not waste your time begging because nothing will make me change my mind." He told the bewildered mother and daughter. They pleaded but he merely hissed and walked out of the house.

Three months after this incident, Egbeide went to Mr. Bibowei Temezigha's house for a follow up on an earlier loan request. The man she knew as Mr. Moneyman a well-known moneylender, ushered her into a small room he used as his office.

"Egbeide, please sit down! I will be with you shortly. The amount you are asking for is not too much. Twenty thousand, is it not?" She nodded.

"I will see what I can do." He promised and left. Emi was in full support of her husband giving Egbeide the money. The couple walked into the office, hand in hand. Stepmother Egbeide on seeing Emi, promptly fainted. When revived, she could only murmur.

"Emi, what are you doing here? Are you Moneyman's wife?"

To all the questions, Emi just smiled and said.

"Yes Mama, I am Bibowei's wife."

At this, Egbeide could only say,

"Aaa! *Aboo! Aboo*! Forgive and forget! Please my daughter, forgive and forget! Oh, please forgive me!"

GLOSSARY

Aboo - *Expression of shock or surprise*

KEME-EKISE

Pere-ere was one of the most beautiful girls in Bulou. As a matter of fact, majority of young men swore that she was the prettiest girl in the entire clan of Oporomo. Pere-ere was so tall and slim that her peers nicknamed her, *'papala!'* In spite of her slimness though, Pere-ere was perfectly shaped. Her long neck effortlessly supported a round head, crowned with luxuriant black hair. A lady's chest is nothing without a good set of breasts and Pere-ere's full breasts were designed to delight men's sense of sight. When she smiled, her thick lips encasing white teeth and big black eyes all come alive, creating an unexplainable energy. Watching her walk, was pure pleasure as her wide hips and well-moulded calves combined to tantalize. Understandably, her beauty attracted men from far and near who used gifts and sweet talk to attract her attention. The long queue of suitors at her parents' three-room un-plastered blockhouse made some of her friends envious.

Meanwhile, Pere-ere was not impressed by all the gifts and praises the various suitors continued to heap on her. To annoyance of parents, she systematically found reasons for refusing all offers of marriage. A lot of people could not help but accuse the young lady of arrogance and pride. Some however, felt that she was not to blame for this seeming indecision because of the sheer number of men seeking her hand in marriage. As time went by though, girls in her age bracket started getting married one after the other. Her parents' anxiety soon turned to despair as it dawned on them that their lovely daughter may never marry. From time to time, the concerned parents would counsel Pere-ere.

"Your beauty is an asset daughter, please do not allow it to go to waste. You cannot remain with us forever so try and make a choice among the many men that want your hand in marriage. We are not blaming you for being confused but please choose one and settle down with that one. We particularly like the one who…"

"Mama! Papa! I am not impressed with any of the men. The two who came yesterday are too short and the one who was here four days ago is like a giant. I cannot marry any of them!" She told them, frowning.

"But Pere-ere, the three that we have seen today look responsible and we were told that…"

"Please Mama, stop this talk! Did you see the shape of the first one's teeth and the brown coloured armpit hair of the second one, not to mention the mountainous belly and loud laughter of the third man? There is no need to be unduly worried. I know you want grandchildren and all that, which is proper. Please be patient with me. I assure you dear parents, that I will get married as soon as the right man appears." She promised.

This was the situation of things when Pere-ere, without knocking bust into her mother and father's bedroom one evening.

"Mama! Papa! HE has finally come!"

"And who is the HE, that is making you smile like this?" Her surprised parents asked.

"O Mama! The man of my dreams, of course! The one I have been waiting for all these years!"

"Oh, this is wonderful news!" Her parents exclaimed.

"Ayiba nua! Let us meet him then!"

Pere-ere practically pulled her parents out of bed to meet the man she considered to be the right one. The excited parents were a bit taken aback though, by what they saw. The light skinned and handsome stranger was sitting in the only cushioned chair reserved for the father of the house! His eyes glowed like those of a cat in the dark and a smile played around his reddish lips. He looked wealthy, judging by the clothes he wore and the gifts he brought. Pere-ere went to him and whispered something. He then stood up and genuflected deeply.

"Papa and Mama, *okoide*! I bring you greetings from Toruama. News of your daughter's beauty reached my ears six months ago and I made up my mind to meet her. Since I was told that men from all over our clan have been coming to your house every day to ask for her hand in marriage, I assumed she had married one of them but I see that she is still single." He said, laughing.

He turned to Pere-ere, looked steadily into her eyes and laughed even louder.

"Come to me my beauty!" he ordered.

Pere-ere obeyed without a word and embraced him.

"You will marry me!" he told her.

"Yes! You are the type of man I have been waiting for!" Pere-ere responded, smiling.

For some unexplainable reason, Pere-ere's parents felt uneasiness creep upon them like the touch of an invisible hand. They told the stranger to come back at a later date for the family's consent.

"Err Mr..."

"O, pardon me please! My name is Keme." He told them laughing.

"We are very happy that our daughter likes you. It is indeed a miracle! She said you are the one for her but since this is our first meeting, we cannot give you a date for the marriage yet. Hmm! You have to come back for..."

"No-o! You have been telling everybody about how I may remain husbandless and now that I have found my dream man, you want to delay everything. No! No! You have to fix the date now!"

"Oo Pere-ere, we are meeting this man for the first time today. Let us at least, have the opportunity of knowing some members of his family before..."

"There is no need for all that. The man has already told us where he is from. You can find out whatever is necessary to know after..."

"It is not done that way my daughter. Please give us some time to investigate." Her father said, almost pleading.

"But Papa, he will come with many of his family members and friends during the marriage. If you do not agree now and this man leaves, I will never accept to marry any other person. I thought you wanted my happiness but I see that..."

"There is no need for lamentations or threats. We can agree on a date now if you insist." The reluctant parents told their daughter.

The delighted Pere-ere hugged her parents together as they settled for the eve of the main market day, a month from the next major market day.

The news of Pere-ere's engagement swept through the village like wild fire. Everyone waited for the big day with anticipation and excitement, while all manner of comments flowed freely.

"So, she has finally agreed to marry! Good for her! I think she is lucky that this man came. She would have become the only beauty without a husband for life! They said the man brought a boatload of gifts. Ahaan! The elders used to say that an extremely choosy spinster always ends up marrying the worst husband but it appears they are wrong this time! Pere-ere is marrying a rich man! Well, let the spirits of her ancestors lead her safely into her new family!"

Pere-ere's wedding day finally arrived and it was like a festival. Bulou had never seen such a group of people and they were awed by the spectacle. The groom came with five boatloads of friends and family. Their attires were so colourful that indigenes of Bulou were convinced that special tailors from a foreign land made them. As for the groom, he was dressed from head to toe in a sparkling white outfit. The only contrast was the blood red coral bead headdress. Mr. Keme spared no expense to ensure that everyone was happy and the ceremony remained in people's memory for a long time. There was so much to eat and drink that many people got drunk, even before the main event started. Live bands played until noon the next day and the venue was so rowdy that a few fights inevitably broke out.

Very early the next morning, Pere-ere's husband woke her up.

"Time to go, my sweet wife, I have already given your parents our home address. Hurry up!"

"Aww! It's too early. I've not even heard the cock, crow. Why the hurry dear husband? Please let's sleep for a while longer. My eyes are not properly open…"

"We must leave without delay. My family and friends are already in their boats and they are waiting for us. Come my sweet, dress up." Pere-ere had no choice but to quickly put on a dress and follow her husband.

She insisted on bidding her parents farewell so Keme reluctantly agreed and waited outside. Not long after the couple's departure, it dawned on Pere-ere's mother that her new son-in-law did not tell her where they would be living. Concerned, she sent someone after them but too late! Their boat had sped off into the early morning mist. When her emissary came back with the news that the couple had gone, she did not worry much. After all, her daughter was a responsible person and would send someone to her parents sooner than later.

Pere-ere was surprised that the two of them were the only ones in their boat and the other boats were not even in sight.

"How could I have allowed other persons travel with us? This is our special time together, my sweet wife. As for my family and friends, they got tired of waiting for us and left."

"I understand my husband. O, I'm so lucky! I did not realise that you are such a powerful and wealthy man... Why are we stopping at this place? Do you want to..."

"Do not worry your beautiful head my love. You will soon find out what type man your husband is."

The happy bride was still busy talking about how lucky she was, when her husband told her to get down from the boat. It dawned on her that they were to walk to their house but she could not see any houses in the distant. She turned to her husband with a question on her lips but he put a finger on her lips. The question was reflected in her eyes and the answer was also clearly stated in his eyes. He took hold of her left hand and they started walking through a narrow bush path. Then a man suddenly appeared and confronted Keme. Pere-ere was taken aback. She looked beyond the man to see if there was a house or even a hut but nothing, only a sea of tall grasses was all she saw. Fear threatened to take hold of the once talkative bride but she managed to keep her composure since Keme was with her.

"Eh, you don't have to be rude! Am I denying that I owe you? You are a good person. Here, take your hands." Baffled, Pere-ere looked from one person to the other and started laughing.

"I know I must be dreaming, right?" She asked her husband. He shook his head firmly.

"Oh no my angel, you are very much awake. Please move on. Home is still far away!"

They walked on in silence for about an hour then suddenly another man ambushed them and asked for his left leg. Without much ado, the groom stretched out the leg. Pere-ere was now numb and beyond speech. She shivered like one in the grip of a deadly fever.

Finally, just before dark they arrived at her husband's home, a one-room thatch hut. They had barely entered the house when two friendly-looking men stopped by. After congratulating the groom for a catch well secured, one asked for his right leg, while the second man asked for his head. Both were thanked and given their properties.

It now became clear to Pere-ere that she was in the biggest trouble any human being could possibly encounter. She was married to a stump of a man! A headless, armless and legless entity! She assumed that she could just trace her way back home and wake up from this horrific nightmare so she furtively looked around and noticed a giant cock under a tree. As she dashed out of the hut, the cock started crowing. Shortly thereafter, the grotesque entity that was her husband pressed her down!

"Where do you think you are running to, my beauty?'

A laugh that sounded like a roar emanated from his belly.

"This is your home now and you better get used to it. You had ample opportunity to marry several decent men but you refused. Reconcile yourself to the fact that you are stuck with me for life!" He advised.

Pere-ere's tears ran down her cheeks like raindrops. Crying became her only pastime and she soon lost her tear glands. She also laughed hysterically now and then to the delight of her amused stump of a husband and his pet cock!

GLOSSARY

Ayiba nua	-	*Thank you God*
Okoide	-	*Genuflecting while greeting an older person*

THREE BROTHERS

There once lived three brothers, whose parents were palm oil merchants. Every so often, the parents would send the brothers to a major market to sell large consignments of processed palm oil. It usually took four days to reach the market. The length of time notwithstanding, the young men enjoyed the journeys because of the extra food provided by their parents. However, when the brothers were sent to the market during the Eremotoru festival, extra food was not given to them. Festive seasons were very demanding and the parents could not spare anything more than basic foodstuff.

"Boys, you know this is a difficult time. I want you to use what I have given you carefully." Their mother cautioned, when she saw them off at the waterfront.

"We understand Mama. I shall ensure that what you have provided is carefully managed. Please do not worry." The eldest son told their mother.

They set out just before dawn. As the journey progressed, the eldest brother warned his siblings.

"Boys, I don't want unnecessary demands for food from any of you. We shall eat only once a day so concentrate on paddling fast. Have you heard me?"

"Yes we have heard you!" The two replied.

The youngest of the brothers was a mere boy, just ten years old. About eight hours into the journey, he started crying.

"O big brother, please give me a little more food. My stomach hurts. Give me food please!" He begged.

"Keep quiet you little fool! Did I not tell you that the food we have is too small to be eaten anyhow? Where you not there when mother advised us to manage the little she was able to give us? You better stop crying. No more food until tomorrow and that is final." He told him sternly.

The boy's cries increased. When all entreaties failed and the cries turned to wails, the angry brother slapped him.

"You better stop disturbing us with your stupid wailing or I will pluck out your eyes before giving you food!" Brother number two was horrified by the threat.

"Please don't say such a thing big brother?" He admonished.

"He is only a little boy. You and I can forego some of our portions for his sake." He reasoned.

"Nonsense! I will do no such thing. I warned you both before we started this journey and now you are telling me stories. Look at the way he is crying as if the world is about to end!" He said, making faces at the boy.

"I will pluck out his eyes and then give him the food he craves. I am not joking."

Big brother stated, yanking the crying boy out of his seat. Before the second brother could intervene, senior brother had forcefully plucked out his eyes! The boy screamed uncontrollably.

"Take the food you have been crying for!" He said handing him a bowl of soup. The dreadful pain prevented the boy from eating the food as he continued to scream.

"O brother, how could you do such a terrible thing? I can't believe it! I thought you were joking! O, this is cruelty at its highest!" Exclaimed the second brother.

He held his now bloody faced little brother, washed his face and tried to pacify him. At long last the boy, whimpering like an injured dog, managed to eat his food. As the journey entered the fourth day, the big brother figured that something more drastic had to be done about their youngest brother. Since he would not be able to give a satisfactory explanation for the boy's sudden blindness, the only option was to come up a foolproof strategy. He took the middle brother to the stern of the boat and in a low tone told him what he was contemplating. Second brother was taken aback and vehemently protested. The objections notwithstanding, big brother argued that the least they could do was to throw the young man overboard. At long last, he succeeded in convincing the now visibly apprehensive brother.

"You will later thank me for this decision. I do not see any way of saving ourselves from the wrath of our parents. You don't have to look as if thunder is about to strike! Trust me, brother."

"Ah! I...I am not easy in my spirit. Eh, I don't want to incur the wrath of the gods... The blood of our little will be on our..."

"Ey my friend! Stop all this stupid talk about the gods and punishment and all that. We had to do what was necessary. No more lamentations please!"

As night fell, the little boy was unceremoniously thrown overboard.

In his innocence, he called out to his brothers for help.

"O, brothers help me! I don't know what is happening. O, help! Help! I am drowning...drowning!" His voice grew fainter and fainter.

Help was nowhere in sight and he grew weaker and weaker until he became unconscious. After what seemed like a very long time, the boy discovered that he was still alive, wedged between two tree stumps. Getting up slowly he started feeling his way through the thick bush, crying and mumbling incoherently. Then, as his hands touched a particular tree, a thunderous male voice asked who he was and what he wanted. He fearfully explained his predicament. The voice then asked.

"Do you want your sight back?"

"Oh yes, Sir!" He answered in a trembling voice.

"I promise not to cry for food again if you restore my sight O, Opu-oru!" He vowed.

"Very well!" Boomed the voice.

"Rub your eyes with the sticky material I am going to drop on your face now!" He instructed.

Moments later, the boy felt a sticky substance drop on his face. He had barely rubbed his face with it when he heard a popping sound. His eyeballs had gotten back into their sockets! The bewildered but happy boy jumped up and down.

"I can see! I can see!" He shouted.

The voice sent him on his way with the substance.

"You will heal others as I have healed you. Go and do not forget this day. Face the sun and keep walking. My spirit is with you. Go in peace."

With a heart full of gratitude, he promised to carry out Opu-oru's instructions.

After several hours of walking, he found himself in a small town called Amabulou. His relief was great, even though he had nowhere to stay. While searching, he saw some people offloading sand at the waterfront and joined the labour line. That was how he began. No assignment or task was too difficult for him. An old woman, whose children had all left home heard his story. She was curious about the boy and sent people to monitor his activities. Finally satisfied with the report, she invited him to live with her. She told him of her decision to adopt him.

"My children are all grown and I am now living alone. I will like to adopt you so you can have a permanent home to call your own."

"Ah! Mama, this is a great honour. I will be very happy to be your son, your last born. I promise not to be a burden to you and I will never give you cause to regret this decision you are making." He told her, genuflecting.

"I know my son. I know." She responded, embracing him.

He moved in almost immediately and the house acquired a new energy that only a youth with good vibrations could bring. The woman had of course, informed her children about the adoption and they were all comfortable with the idea because of the circumstances that led the boy to their village. His lively and cheerful nature endeared him to everyone in the community. The imperceptive hands of time touch all of humanity and no time at all it seemed, the little boy of yesterday was now a young man of nineteen.

While working at a building site one day, he learnt that the traditional ruler of a neighbouring village had problems with his eyes. According to his informant, the kingdom's ruler could no longer see and had to be assisted in almost everything. Recalling the advice of Opu-oru who restored his sight, he immediately offered to cure the old man.

"Please my friend, take me to the ruler. I think I can help." He said. His fellow labourer laughed outright.

"What a joke! Look at the person talking. Please, concentrate on your work." He advised.

An old man passing by overheard this conversation and called the young man aside. After a brief discussion, he promised to take him to the king. It was with great excitement that he followed the old man to the neighbouring kingdom the next day. The matter was first discussed with the chief spokesman of the kingdom.

"Are you sure of the young man's abilities? We do not want experimenters and false herbalists in our community so you better be sure of what you are saying." The spokesman told them.

"But you know me. Have I ever associated myself with anything other than that, which is genuine? You of all people should..."

"My sincere apologies wise one. I forget myself at times it seems. Please forgive me. I should take you to the king as soon as the dignitaries from kpakiama leave the palace."

A wait of about four hours followed, after which the young man was taken before the king. The Ruler was sceptical and not at all impressed but when the spokesman told him that the young man was brought by the wise one from Amabulou, he relaxed and smiled.

"In that case young man, if your claim is true and I regain my sight two thirds of my kingdom will be yours. I am an old man as you can see and the immense wealth I have will outlive me. No greater joy will I have than giving it to someone who contributes to the enjoyment of my old age." He said.

"O, good King! Opu-oru gave me a charge when he restored my sight. Go into the world and help others as I have helped you. I believe in the efficacy of Opu-oru's medicine because in me is the proof. Turn your face towards me please." He told him. The ruler's eyes were then thoroughly rubbed with the sticky substance.

"A miracle! A miracle! I can see! I see you and you and you!" The king shouted, moving from one person to another. He laughed and embraced the young man.

The overjoyed king kept his promise and shared his assets with the young man who subsequently became one of the most influential persons in the entire clan. He eventually became the traditional ruler of the kingdom.

Many years passed before fate brought the brothers together again. Their parents were already very old when war broke out between their community and a neighbouring town. Incidentally, the war was with the community ruled by none other than their discarded brother. The fighting was fierce and several persons were captured. It so happened that the two brothers were among those captured. All prisoners were taken before the ruler who immediately recognized his brothers. As commander-in-chief, he ordered that the fighting be stopped without further delay. Subsequently, a joint peace meeting was called where the ruler briefed his top advisers about his dilemma. The council told him to reveal his true identity to his brothers and unanimously agreed that the older brother be sentenced to death. The second brother begged for mercy and council elders deliberated on his plea for a long time. One man argued that both brothers should be put to death.

"If you advise the ear and it ignores the advice, it will surely be cut off with the head, when circumstances call for such!" The man said, hissing. Finally though, the council voted to spare the life of brother number two. The aged parents were later reunited with their son and what a great reunion it was!

GLOSSARY

Opu-oru   -   *Great god*

UNLIKELY HERO

"Wuu wuu! Run everybody! Hide your children! Lock your doors! This is the town crier speaking!"

Usually when such a proclamation is made, the town becomes a virtual ghost settlement. Even the pigs, goats and fowls would be found hiding under elevated bamboo houses.

Inhabitants of KOLOBA, a sleepy rural town lived in the grip of a terrorizing man-eating animal. None of the so-called strong men who were fond of boasting about their power and prowess, had the courage to face the fearsome beast. In fact, they were the first to run into their houses as dusk approached. It looked as though Koloba people were condemned to lives of uncertainty. They resigned themselves to fate and many rationalized their situation by proffering all kinds of theories from the absurd to the probable.

"The sins of our ancestors are catching up with us and there's nothing we can do about it!" Claimed some.

"It is most likely the work of the devil and his cohorts, supported by our own witches and wizards!" Others chipped in.

Many just sighed and threw up their arms, a clear sign of helplessness or hopelessness. Parents did not get tired of warning their children and wards from going out at night for any reason whatsoever. Defecating into paper bags in their rooms was preferable to being devoured by the wild animal they reasoned.

"Is it not true that he who lives near the devil understands his language? Why tempt fate?" Questioned Egiren the leader of Endidou Ogbo women cooperative.

This was the situation in Koloba when citizen Gboro's young nephew Bebebi came to visit her. Since the story or to put it more accurately, the reality of the man-eating animal was well known all over the region, the young guest needed no special information. All the same, to satisfy her conscience Gboro went over some basic safety precautions and rules with her nephew.

"You must lock the door when it is dark. Don't open the door at night, no matter who knocks. Please my child, in your own interest do not forget what I have just told you!" She warned.

"Please don't worry about me, I will be careful." Bebebi assured her.

The household was quiet. The firewood in the kitchen had burnt out and the ashes scattered around the fireside. Bebebi, in spite of Gboro's admonitions decided to go outside for some fresh air. The sound of a creaking door instantly alerted Gboro who quickly lighted the oil lamp and looked around, just as Bebebi was about to step outside. She begged him not to go but he merely smiled and told her not to worry and slipped through the door before she could utter another word.

"O, what foolishness! O *Temearau*! What will I tell my brother ehh that I could not look after his son?" The distressed woman sighed, pacing up and down. Meanwhile, young Bebebi went to the main thoroughfare by the waterfront and lit a huge fire. He collected the six iron rods he earlier hid behind his aunt's house and threw them into the blaze and waited. He didn't have long to wait as a gigantic creature appeared just a few yards from him, apparently attracted by the fire.

"How dare you light a fire in the dark?" It roared.

"Have you not heard about the man eater? I will teach you a bitter lesson, you foolish boy! You will see the land of the ghosts shortly!" It threatened at the same time, moving towards Bebebi.

"We shall see!" He replied as the animal charged at him. Bebebi immediately threw one of the rods into beast's wide-open mouth. The shocked animal stopped momentarily, thereby giving Bebebi the opportunity to throw the remaining five rods at it in quick succession. He did not wait to see the outcome of his effort but ran back to his aunt's house. Gboro could not believe her eyes when Bebebi rushed in. She wanted to question him but he refused to talk and went straight to bed. The woman was so thankful that she just turned and went back to her room.

Early next morning, inhabitants were woken by shouts.

"*Aboo! Aboo! Eh! Koloba!* Wake up everyone!"

People hurriedly got out of bed and rushed to the waterfront. There was bewilderment, mixed with relief. The dreaded killer beast lay dead in a mountainous heap! The entire community gathered to gape at the animal. Everyone wanted to know who killed it. Elders and community leaders held an emergency meeting and announced that the killer of the terrorizer would be rewarded. All royalties accruing to the community from its raffia palm leases would be shared in two, with one half going to the hero. The town crier called on everyone to ask questions and find the saviour of the community. Several hours went by and the hero could still not be found. Then, the town's spokesman pointed to a tattered sandal lying close to the dead animal.

"Let us find the owner of this shoe. It may belong to the hero." He suggested.

There was a frenzy of activity as parents tried to fit their children's feet into the shoe. Gboro recalled the nocturnal outing of her nephew and marched him to the town square. She took hold of his right foot and pushed it into the shoe and behold it was a perfect fit! There was thunderous applause! Indeed, a knife knows the belly of the fish to enter! Bebebi's bravery and courage earned him an income for life. He became a wealthy person until the day he died.

GLOSSARY

Aboo!	-	*Expression of surprise/wonder*
Temearau	-	*God*
Wuu wuu!	-	*Expression for urgent attention*

TIGER AND GOAT

Many, many years ago, the ruler of the animal kingdom decreed that animals everywhere must meet at least once a year. The reason for this decree was simple. Word had reached him that several smaller animals were being severely oppressed by the big ones. As a benevolent and humane ruler who believed in the equality of all animals, he felt certain only close interaction between the different types of animals would bring peace and happiness to the animal world. All the animals hailed their ruler's decision because he was known for making wise choices in matters of world interest.

During the maiden annual conference of animals in the Africa continental zone, many interesting firsts were recorded. One of the most noteworthy was the friendship of a Goat and a Tiger. The excited new friends invited their wives and informed them about the development. Goat's wife was not pleased at all in fact, she was angry. On the other, Tiger's wife was happy. She embraced Mrs. Goat warmly.

"O, this is a great day! I am sure two of us and our children will form a lasting bond of friendship." She said, smiling.

"Ar...you are right! This is indeed a wonderful day." Mrs. Goat responded, scratching the ground. When they got home, she told her husband he had made a serious mistake.

"I will not support a friendship between you and Tiger, never! Everyone knows that he is..."

"Ah my dear wife, don't you think I know what Tiger is capable of? Trust me, it is in our interest that I befriend him. Our world leader who initiated this annual conference knows what he is doing. He wants to prove a very important point."

"Which is?"

"The common ancestry of all animals, even though we are compelled to hunt for the nourishment of our bodies. That we are shaped differently does not remove the fact that we are all basically animals. By the time we make friends with each other and interact without fear our hidden strengths will become manifest, thereby promoting mutual respect."

He was so persuasive that she finally accepted the idea. Meanwhile, Mrs Tiger congratulated her husband for being true to their world leader's idealistic posture by befriending Goat. She was so happy that barely one week after the conference, she invited Mr and Mrs Goat to dine with them. As the two couples were enjoying their meal, Mr Goat turned to his host with a big smile.

"Tiger my friend, how are we going to operate our friendship?"

"Oh simple! We should each hunt separately and later share the meat equally. However, the first hunt should be a joint one. What do you say, my dear friend?" Tiger asked, also smiling.

"O, very agreeable! I like the arrangement!" Goat responded, looking at his wife.

They shared jokes and laughed heartily. Both families agreed that the dinner was successful and expressed the hope that their friendship would be an enduring one. A date for the first joint hunt was agreed upon before Mr. and Mrs. Goat departed.

One week after the dinner, the friends met at the appointed place and set out for what promised to be a rewarding adventure. Before Mr Goat left home however, he expressed some apprehension and confided in his wife that Mr Tiger's intentions were suspect but pride would not allow him back out of the friendship. She encouraged him to stay in the relationship, reminding him of their world leaders charge that there should be openness among animals.

"Just be alert. I believe all will be well. Remember, you are the one who convinced me about the importance of this friendship when I objected."

With his wife's assurances still sounding in his ears, Goat followed Tiger into the dense forest.

"Why don't we meet under that Indian bamboo tree in two hours?" Tiger suggested.

"Good idea my friend!" Goat agreed as they went into different parts of the forest.

Barely one hour after the hunt began, Tiger had caught so much game that he headed back to the meeting point. When he got to the place he discovered that Goat had not returned, so he neatly arranged all the game and waited. After two hours of waiting, he was just contemplating going in search of Goat when he saw him coming out empty handed, head bowed. Tiger ran to his friend and assured him that there was enough meat for them to share.

"Eh my man, don't look so depressed. I caught enough game for our two families. What are friends for?" He asked.

With a heart full of sadness, Goat accompanied his friend back home and the meat was shared equally among them. Two months later, it was the turn of Tiger to hunt alone. He did such a marvellous job that both families decided to sell the excess meat after sharing. When it got to the turn of Goat to hunt, he quietly went into the forest and started crying. He cried so much that his tears not only wet his chest but his stomach and legs as well! The weeping was so loud that Bouosuo-wei, the mighty spirit of the forest was waken from sleep.

"Who dares disturb the thorn of the forest? Don't you know that the keeper of forest fire rests?" A thunderous voice asked. Goat explained his predicament.

"I am so ashamed mighty wind of the forest that I cannot kill even a small rat to present to my partner, Tiger. Oh Great Spirit, help me if you can! I cannot face my friend if I fail again." He groaned.

Bouosuo-wei took pity on him and assisted him kill ten times the number of animals his friend killed, including a baby elephant. Goat's joy knew no bounds as he gathered all the game and went home.

Mr and Mrs Tiger and even his wife were astonished. As Tiger's turn drew near, he sent his wife to Mrs Goat to find out the secret of her husband's success.

"Do not ask in a direct way. No need to arouse suspicion. You are a clever woman please do not disappoint me."

"I will do my best. Do not be bothered, my husband." Tiger was reassured after his wife's confident remarks.

Mrs Goat was a bit surprised to see Mrs Tiger very early one morning. Nonetheless, the friends embraced and asked after each other's families. Though Mrs Tiger did not openly state the reason for her visit, Mrs Goat was not at all fooled. She thought fast and like a hunch-backed woman who devices a method of sleeping with her husband, she came up with an ingenious response. She told Mrs Tiger that her husband had entered into a pact with the mighty spirit of the forest. The implication of this was that Mr Goat had become a consecrated being whose face, people like Tiger could no longer look upon again.

"I can tell you categorically that anyone who looks into my husband's eyes would be shocked to death without warning! Bouosuo-wei is known to deal decisively with those who disobey him." She emphasized.

Mrs Tiger delivered this chilling message to her husband who promptly terminated their friendship!

EWIRI AND LEDENE

"It is a fact! Why are you arguing with me! All right thinking persons know this or are you saying that..."

"What do you mean? So I am a fool, eh?"

"You are the one calling yourself a fool. All I am saying is that Ewiri's wisdom is yet to be matched by any living being."

"You mean cunning?"

"Eh! You are entitled to your opinion and I, to mine."

The above conversation took place between Toru and Bebe. There was hardly anywhere one went in the kingdom of Beni that such debates were not taking place.

It so happened once upon a time, that this same Ewiri of Beni decided to embark on business trips to some far away kingdoms.

"I shall be travelling to these kingdoms when the moon stands firm in the middle of the sky. My periodic interaction with those people will bring prosperity to our land." He told the elders of Beni who were quite impressed with his presentation.

"May our ancestors and the gods of the land continue to bless you!" They told him. The journeys usually took three days.

"I am a generous and caring person as you all know. My primary concern at this point in my life is the empowerment of our young people. To this effect, one of your sons should be nominated to accompany me during every trip." The grateful parents would happily give him one of their sons to serve as his apprentice.

To ensure that the lucky apprentice was not in doubt about his functions during the trip, Ewiri would organize a brief lecture on the eve of their departure.

"Listen very carefully to all my instructions my son. It is important that we arm ourselves with at least a knife as well as a sharpener. Now, you are to keep the knife sharpener in your bag. I will let you know when it will be needed to sharpen the knife."

"Yes Papa Ewiri! I will do as instructed." The apprentice would respond enthusiastically.

There were three mandatory stops during such journeys to enable travellers eat and replenish their stock. Ewiri routinely sent his apprentices on errands during these meal breaks. The tasks were such that by the time the boy returned, mealtime was over. Master Ewiri would then scold the apprentice for being sluggish!

"Well, since the food is finished you better drink as much water as you can. Take this cup of water and drink up!" He would order. This was the standard practice.

With so much water drinking, the apprentice's stomach would swell like that of a pregnant pig. On their return home, parents of the boy would mistake bloatedness for plumpness and greet Ewiri effusively. About three boys were treated this way and all eventually died. Ewiri was never blamed instead, curses were heaped on envious neighbours.

Then a fifteen-year old boy named Ledene, volunteered to travel with Ewiri when the harmattan winds were at their strongest. Beni indigenes fondly referred to Ledene as, '*short boy tall pass man!*' He was three feet tall and had hairs all over his body. His teeth resembled those of a roasted goat and his eyes were always bloodshot.

"Papa Ewiri! I am very impressed with the way you feed your assistants. Please let me go with you this time. You know I am from a poor family and everyone in Beni knows that you are a philanthropist. Surely, you cannot refuse to assist a struggling boy like me?" He said, kneeling at Ewiri's feet.

Ewiri preferred to have parents beg on behalf of their sons. He did not like young people who were forward, so his first instinct was to refuse Ledene's request. He looked at the eager face of the young man keeling at his feet and could not refuse because people were watching.

"My dear boy! Of course, I cannot refuse! I will be glad to help you. After all, my mission is to contribute to the progress of my community. I know you are very poor. Get ready to accompany me!" He stated.

Ledene packed his little bag and waited expectantly. On the appointed day, Ewiri sent someone to fetch Ledene and they set out after the usual instructions. As they got to the first stop, Ledene brought out the sharpener and stood by his master. Ewiri glared at him but the young boy would not move.

"Did you not hear me? I said you should go the market we just passed and buy tobacco for me. Ask for Madam Kakakon and tell her I sent you. Search the entire market place if you do not see her near the coconut tree."

"A responsible apprentice must always stand close to his master Papa Ewiri. I cannot leave you here all alone. What if thieves attack you? The whole of Beni will blame me. You are a bad boy Ledene, they will say. O, Papa of the youth, please don't send me to Madam Kakakon at this time." He told his master.

Ewiri was not at all amused. When it was time to eat, Ewiri had no choice than to invite the spunky Ledene to eat with him. The same thing happened at the second stop. Ewiri was so infuriated that he terminated the trip and returned home. Needless to say, that was the end of Ewiri's 'humanitarian' journeys!

GLOSSARY

Ewiri   -   *Tortoise.*

ROPE AROUND OYINBRA

"Papa, Mama, I have found him!" Exclaimed Ebisine, as she ran excitedly through the door to her parents living quarters.

"Who have you found eh? Why this noise eh?" asked Kro, Ebisine's father irritably haven been woken from a dream-filled afternoon nap.

"Oh Papa, he is so handsome, so sharp, so delightful…….."

"Enough!" he barked.

"Allow me enjoy my sleep in peace, ah! Running in here as if the great Osuopele masquerade himself, was after you!"

Meanwhile, Maki her mother bounced out of the kitchen.

"My husband, why are you such a mean man? Ahuu! *Apoo*! Always grumbling like a dog whose favourite bone has been forcefully taken from it. Be happy when someone brings good news."

Turning to Ebisine she asked,

"Did you say you have found the person hmm? Tell me everything my child. When did it all start?"

She pulled her daughter into her sweaty bosom dancing merrily, while demanding that all details be quickly given. Ebisine happily narrated everything concluding,

"I am truly blessed Mama. Nemi is so responsible and caring. Really Mama, you couldn't wish for a better son-in-law." Maki beamed.

"O! Thank God! *Oyin nua-o!*" She repeated over and over, eyes looking skyward.

"When are you bringing him, to meet us?" She asked.

Ebisine took her mother's hand, pulled her aside and whispered conspiratorially. Maki's booming laughter jolted her husband who had gone back to his interrupted siesta. Now fully awake, he strolled over to his wife and daughter who were talking animatedly. Wanting to be part of the excitement, he was more conciliatory this time when he asked to be briefed about his daughter's 'good news.' Ebisine was only too happy to inform her father about her newfound love. She told him about Nemi, a young man from a very good family.

"I met him about a year ago. He is a very nice and responsible person Papa. He has expressed his readiness to begin marriage formalities as soon as you and mama give your consent," she said, smiling.

Kro and his wife could hardly contain their joy as they listened attentively. They asked a few questions about Nemi's ancestry. Satisfied with the answers, the delighted parents gave their approval for Nemi to start the traditional '*Warinemi Esomo.*'

Ebisine was anxious to tell Nemi about her parent's approval of their proposed marriage. She therefore excused herself from the family meeting and went over to his house. The excited Nemi drew his heartthrob into a close embrace and gave her a lingering kiss.

"So, I can now activate my plans?" He demanded.

"Yes of course! This is what I have been telling you since I got here. I thought you were listening!"

They laughed unrestrainedly like two children sharing a secret.

"Nemnem dear," Ebisine called softly, suddenly serious.

"I want to give you a house-full of children and it is my wish to become a mother by the time I turn twenty."

"O my sweet Ebisine, I love you so much. I shall endeavour to conclude the ceremony in three months, so we can be together always. I want to spend the rest of my life with you. This is my promise to you." he said, holding the side of her head with warm palms and touching her forehead with his lips.

He kept his word and in three months flat, they had become husband and wife. There was great rejoicing in the families of Kro Agom and Bunuzigha Ditmi, all of Bulou-ozobo town. Although Nemi's parents were initially sceptical about Ebisine, their doubts vanished when they investigated the young lady's background. It was discovered that her parents were humble and God-loving, bringing up all their children according to a strict moral code. Above all, Ebisine was reputed to have high moral standards and always displayed the attributes of someone with common sense.

Several women wanted her to marry their sons. So understandably Ebiakpo, Nemi's mother, became the envy of all the scheming mothers.

"*Apoo*! What a lucky woman this Ebiakpo is," some of them said. They could not just stop talking about the marriage.

"How did she do it? Imagine! She did not even struggle or make any special effort like us. Maybe it is that God of hers she keeps calling all the time that did it," they reasoned.

"It's okay" one of the sober ladies chipped in.

"It is her luck that the best daughter-in-law any woman could hope for has become hers. Let us be happy for her," she advised with finality.

A few months after their marriage, Nemi and Ebisine were compelled to move to a bigger town, Agbere because of better job opportunities. An oil-prospecting firm discovered a large deposit of crude oil and the subsequent construction of a flow-station in Agbere territory made the town a hob of activities. The young couple took advantage of this change to broaden their horizons. They made friends easily and became a fixture in the community's social circles. Married life was good for them and they eagerly looked forward to starting a family.

Nemi consoled his wife when she complained about not becoming pregnant a year after marriage. He noted that a year was too short a time for her to start worrying. Time went by quickly and before Ebitimi realised what was happening, five years had gone by and she was still childless! To make matters worse, her mother-in-law had started dropping hints. She was reliably informed that even her father-in-law who loved her dearly, advised his son to marry a second wife. In fact, her own parents too were anxious to 'carry' their grandchild. The pressure was immense and she became desperate. The ordinarily vivacious Ebisine became drawn and haggard. She was weepy and irritable. Luckily, Nemi remained steadfast and always encourage his wife to be hopeful. This loving husband's solid support drove despair away from Ebisine.

He showered her with surprise gifts every now and then. His attitude made life bearable and she was very grateful. The numerous conventional and traditional conception-inducing remedies they continued to try did not help at all. At long last it dawned on them that some kind of decision had to be made about their situation. It was significant that their tenth wedding anniversary was just a few weeks away. Several friends had suggested adoption but this option was unattractive to them. A number of orthodox and traditional doctors had confirmed that they found no medical reason for the couple's inability to have children. There was no reason therefore to consider adoption, the couple reasoned. For weeks, Nemi and his wife pondered a cause of action. However, the more options they considered, the more appealing the adoption idea looked.

"If it will make you happy my dear, I am all for adoption," Nemi finally said.

"I can't bear to see you unhappy."

It was the extra push Ebisine needed and she gratefully acquiesced.

"A girl is my first choice, if you do not mind dear."

"Of course my darling, anything that will make you happy, will make me even happier" was Nemi's immediate response.

In no time at all, the now invigorated couple located a government approved orphanage and enlisted their names. After a year's wait, they adopted a beautiful abandoned girl, aged three. The little girl adapted quickly and Ebisine forgot her initial problems. She dotted on her new child, whom they named Oyinbra. Nemi was every inch the proud father as he showed her off at every opportunity.

Since Nemi and his wife had a good source of income, they sent Oyinbra to one of the best schools in their neighbourhood. This happy atmosphere enveloped not only the contented parents but their friends as well. For no apparent reason it seemed, Ebisine's friend Perefadei started 'advising' the new mother against the temptation to maltreat Oyinbra. Ebisine loathed such advice and was offended by her friend's needless meddlesomeness.

"Why on earth would I abuse my own child or use her as a 'house girl' as you seem to imply by the cynical manner you phrased your so-called 'advice'?" She demanded angrily.

Being a mature person, Perefadei readily apologized.

"My friend, I'm sorry if I have offended you. I did not mean what I said in a bad way. Abeg, no vex", she whispered and walked away. Something in her friend's manner made Perefadei uncomfortable but she shrugged off her unease.

About five years after Oyinbra's adoption, Nemi lost his job and he was devastated. Ebisine assured him of her ability to comfortably shoulder the family's responsibilities until he found another employment. She told him that the business he opened for her had improved greatly since she added dressmaking and sale of jewellery. Nemi was grateful that he had such a responsible and industrious wife. She proved to be such a strong shock absorber that in less than two months, he had overcome his frustration. Their standard of living remained the same and Nemi had the added joy of spending quality time with his beloved Oyinbra, who had blossomed into a fine little lady.

On the down side however, was Ebisine's high blood pressure which was caused by the stress of her increased workload. This turn of events made her husband uneasy and he doubled his job hunting efforts. His diligence notwithstanding, he is still hadn't found work a year after. Like child's play his situation remained unchanged and three years after, he was still distributing resumes from office to office. He decided at this point to join his wife's business on a full basis, instead of just assisting occasionally. Ebisine wholeheartedly welcomed this development.

As he reported for work one morning, Ebisine invited him to meet a friend Doctor Fun-ebi, who handed Nemi a sheet of paper and asked him to read it. Slightly baffled, he read the contents and screamed. When he recovered his composure, speech deserted him as tears flowed freely.

The paper contained a pregnancy test result of his wife! Ebisine had finally conceived after several years of marriage! He got up in a daze and embraced his wife so tightly that she cried in mock horror.

"Eh my darling, you are squashing us-o!"

Nemi was instantly contrite, fearing that he may have inadvertently harmed the unborn baby. Turning to Doctor Fun-ebi, he asked fearfully.

"Eh Doc, hope no harm has been done to the baby. O, how thoughtless of me!"

Fun-ebi and Ebisine laughed hilariously. The doctor assured him that no harm had been done. Nemi exhaled and joined the general laughter.

The happy couple locked up their shop for the day to celebrate the happy news. When they got home, Oyinbra was duly informed and educated about her expected sibling and she was delirious with joy.

"Oh! Daddy, Mummy! A baby brother for me! I am so happy! I have a name already," she gushed.

"if it is a girl, her name will be..."

"Eh small madam, hold on!" Ebisine said, laughing.

"Take it easy. The three of us will sit down and compare names later, okay!"

"Yes, yes Mummy!" agreed Oyinbra breathlessly, rushing off to write down her names murmuring, 'girl, girl, girl!'

All their friends were also duly informed and Perefade was especially happy at the good news. She thanked the Almighty for finally answering her friend's prayers and wished her a trouble-free pregnancy.

Ebisine was rushed to the community health centre as soon as she started having labour pains. Nemi fainted once he heard his wife's loud screams. Finally, the long-awaited baby arrived, born at midnight. The child, a boy was named Powei, to reflect the boundless joy of his parents. Oyinbra was the perfect little mother and was very protective of her baby brother. As expected, the excited parents hosted their friends and family to a lavish naming and thanksgiving ceremony. Their cup of happiness was full it seemed. What more could they complain about? Their business was going on well and they were reasonably comfortable. Then, two years after powei's birth, Ebisine's shop was completely razed in a midnight fire that engulfed the entire market complex. Everything the couple owned went up with the flames.

They were in dire straits and understandably distraught.

"What are we going to do now?" Ebisine asked her husband, who was totally and completely shattered by the huge loss they had suffered.

"Oh my darling, I wish I knew what to do, how to start rebuilding! I sincerely wish we had saved more when we had the opportunity," he sighed.

Their savings did not amount to much because they always reinvested any profit they made.

"Well, now that we are this situation, we must raise some money somehow to rebuild the business. There are banks or money lenders…"

"Stop my dear!" Nemi screamed.

"Money lenders are deadly. Don't ever stray into any money lenders' tent. As for banks, you know how stiff their conditions are but we can still try," he concluded.

When they eventually decided to borrow, the bank requested for collateral which they could not provide. In a matter of months, this fairly well-to-do couple had been reduced to selling 'pure water.' The first 'victim' of this downturn in the family's fortunes was Oyinbra. She was withdrawn from school and 'employed' as a pure water sales girl. Perefadei was saddened by her friend's misfortune. She was particularly apprehensive about Oyinbra's hawking because of the dangers this form of exposure posed to children, especially girls.

One day, Oyinbra went to sell water in a quite part of the town, calling out 'puu-rr-ee waa-ter!' in a sing song manner.

Some thirsty looking workers at a construction site offered to buy and she dutifully approached to sell them the chilled water. As soon as she put down the bucket, one of the men forcefully pull her into an empty room. Oyinbra struggled and shouted but no one came to her aid. The man subsequently raped her. She was distraught and threw her herself on the ground wailing.

"Aw God! My God! What have I done to this wicked man to deserve this treatment? Eei somebody help me!" She cried dejectedly.

At this point, a friend of the rapist threatened her.

"You useless girl, will you shout up and go away from this place! Run off before I beat you up, foolish girl. Common! Get away quickly Abi you wan die? If you tell anybody, na die be that-o! I think you hear me well, well? If you talk ehn…," he warned ominously.

Oyinbra fearfully muffed her cries and ran unsteadily out of the premises then stopped briefly when she noticed blood tricking down her thigh. She cleaned the blood with her bare hands as best as she could then walked home slowly because of the pain she felt both physically and psychologically. Terribly traumatized by the whole experience she sobbed, muttering,

"How will I tell mummy and daddy? Oh what will I do? I don't want this evil me to kill me. I must keep quite even though I'm in pain," she told herself.

Misery consumed her whole being and she looked like a whipped kitten.

A few months after this incident, Oyinbra started showing signs of depression. She became sluggish and was not even interested in playing with her little brother. Ebitimi took notice of the girl's unusual behaviour and asked what was wrong. After a number of probing questions, the truth came to light. Oyinbra was pregnant! The construction site rapist had impregnated the hapless young lady! The revelation was too much for Ebisine to bear, which some believe informed her uncharacteristic reaction. She held her head and screamed like a woman bitten by the village mad man.

"Get out of my house with your bastard. Who would have thought you of all people will be running after boys at your age! God forgive me but I am happy that you are not my real flesh and blood. There is no way I can keep you under my roof anymore," she told the crying girl.

Oyinbra pleaded and begged for forgiveness but Ebisine could not be appeased. She pushed the now wailing girl out of the compound.

"It is not my fault Mummy. Please forgive me. The men said they wanted... to buy water...I was...afraid to tell you and daddy because the wicked man promised...to kill me...and..."

"I say get away from this compound," fumed an incensed Ebisine, throwing stones at Oyinbra.

Now faced with destitution, the poor girl ran to the house of Perefadei, her mother's bosom friend. On reaching there, Oyinbra, still crying and breathless told her,

"Aunty Perefadei, it is not my fault-o! I was just selling the pure water when some men called me. I thought they wanted to buy," she said, tears now flowing freely.

"I know my dear. It is alright. Everything will be fine. Now tell me everything. What is the matter? What did you do? Did you steal something or injured the baby or get into a fight or....,"

"No, no!" Oyinbra said, shaking her head vigorously from side to side.

"Aunty, this is what happened."

After listening attentively, Perefadei shook her head in disbelief. It was inconceivable that Ebisine could throw the child out of her home. She considered this a callous act by her friend and promised to do something about it.

"I will talk to your parents and make sure that those dangerous men are arrested and jailed. They cannot be allowed to do this to other children. A lion on the loose must be captured and caged before it devours innocent persons, so it must be with those rapists."

On hearing this statement, Oyinbra almost fainted.

"I beg you aunty, please don't do that. They said I will be a dead girl if I talk. Aunty, the men promised to kill me," she sobbed.

This good woman, overcome with compassion for this innocent victim, accommodated her. Determined to see justice done, Perefadei went to Ebitimi's house. She burst in without knocking and chastised her friend before appealing to her not to abandon Oyinbra.

"Need I remind you of your promise Ebitimi. You are not the friend I thought I knew," Perefadei shouted.

"But then again, I am not too surprised. When I advised you years ago not to maltreat Oyinbra, you got angry and said so many unprintable things to me. Have I not been proven right eh? Look at how you are behaving. It is as if the whole world has come down on you. I am begging you and you are not even listening. Where do you think this poor child will end up if you refuse to take her back?

"Please, in all my life........."

"Enough! Madam goodie, goodie! I say enough of this preaching!" barked Ebitimi.

"The wayward child can take her pregnancy to the man or boy or whoever impregnated her. I am not having a bastard in my house. The stubborn fly must surely be buried with the corpse......"

Just as she wanted to continue, Perefadei cut in.

"You this woman, are you deaf and dumb? Did Oyinbra not tell you that she was raped? Or are you so caught up in righteous anger that you are not even interested in investigating the child's claim?"

She might as well have been appealing to a brick wall. But suddenly, Ebitimi exploded.

"Look Madam, I am not at all interested please go away, now!"

Perefadei's spirit dropped and she bared her teeth like those of a clown on road show. Seething with anger, she lambasted her erstwhile friend.

"It is people like you, who cause the increase and prevalence of child abuse and rape in this country. This poor child is a victim of circumstance who deserves our support and understanding. You should be going after the offenders and getting them arrested, prosecuted and jailed. Your insensitivity has made Oyinbra a double victim," she hissed.

Leaving Ebisine in annoyance, Perefadei made up her mind to take care of Oyinbra, though she was in need of financial support herself. When Oyinbra was told that her parents had completely disowned her, the child cried brokenly until the tears dried on her face.

"Aw aunty, it is not true. My mummy and daddy cannot disown me. It is a lie, a lie!" she sobbed.

"I have no other person in this world. Where will I go? Where will I live eh, aunty?" she asked.

"Do not worry Oyinbra. I will take care of you from now on," replied Perefadei.

"But you are only managing. At least, that is what you used to tell my mummy, so how can you add my problem to yours," Oyinbra questioned between tears.

"Oh my wise little one," Perefadei managed a weak smile.

"It appears you have matured overnight. Do not mind what I said to your mummy. The good Lord will take care of us…. He will surely provide," she finished confidently.

"But what did my daddy say? Maybe he will help us eh?" Oyinbra asked hopefully.

"I do not think so my dear."

"Your father has disappointed me greatly. I sincerely thought he was a man of good conscience but this is not the case. I'm so sorry that he has not behaved like an educated man concerned with social, family and civic responsibilities. Do not be troubled little one, we will get by," she assured.

Perefadei battled with the twin emotions of disgust and frustration as she watched Oyinbra cry herself to sleep. It seemed as if she did not have the ability to console the broken hearted child but eventually, calm was restored.

The pregnancy was difficult for Oyinbra as she was plagued by nausea, almost daily. She was miserable and could not understand why her early mornings were dominated by vomiting. Perefadei assured the expectant mother about the normalness of vomiting during pregnancy. Her new guardian could not afford to send her for anti-natal care but rather arranged with a local woman for occasional massages and administration of some time-tested herbal remedies.

"My little mother-to-be, what you are experiencing is called morning sickness. As a matter of fact, the easiest way to know whether a girl is pregnant is how often she vomits. So now, we are doubly sure that you are really and truly pregnant!" she teased. Oyinbra did not find her condition funny at all and sighed heavily.

"O! Aunty, I wish there was a better way! Frankly, the vomiting makes me so weak and I lose appetite too. What will I do? Can you make the vomiting go away aunty?"

She sobbed, tears running down her ruddy cheeks. Seeing the tears and how unhappy and lost Oyinbra looked, Perefadei's heart ached. All she could do was gather this forlorn creature into her warm bosom, rock her gently, while singing her a lullaby.

"Don't you worry, baby girl

This will soon pass

You will hold your baby

Your little baby girl

To suckle

Suckle, suckle, your baby Oyinbra

Don't you worry, baby girl

This will soon pass."

Thus, it became a habit of Perefadei's to sing Oyinbra to sleep. Little wonder then that Oyinbra became more relaxed and happy, helping out with household chores as best she could. Perefadei was never tired of exclaiming,

"What a blessing you are! I am so happy to have you around little Oyinbra!"

At long last, Oyinbra's due date arrived and she went into labour. For two agonizing days, the poor girl laboured in the true sense of the word. She bore the labour pains stoically in order not to alarm her guardian unduly. Wise beyond her years she even managed a few weak smiles now and then, encouraging her 'adopted mother' not to panic.

"I will be okay. God will help aunty."

By the time Perefadei borrowed enough money from neighbours to take the pregnant girl to hospital, both mother and child had reached distress stage. Guardian and ward were now crying bitterly at the sad turn events, though Perefadei continued to encourage Oyinbra.

"Oh, my baby it will be okay. Don't cry Oyinbra. It is okay. All will be well," she cooed, while discretely wiping tears from her own eyes.

Doctors battled for hours to save Oyinbra after successfully delivering her of a weak but breathing baby girl. Finally though, they lost the battle as Oyinbra died peacefully, not even realizing that she had brought a beautiful baby girl into the world.

Perefadei was so bitter that she did not even bother to inform her erstwhile friends Ebisine and Nemi about what happened to Oyinbra. She managed to sell some of her wrappers to raise money for the burial, while sympathizers also contributed what they could.

After the burial, Perefadei was faced with the dilemma of what to do with Oyinbra's child. She consulted the hospital authorities who advised her to take the baby to the government orphanage if she could not afford to raise it. With a heavy heart, this 'grandmother' of circumstance took the baby to the orphanage. However, she made the officials promise that the child must be named Oyin-nemi, to reflect the circumstances of her birth and the way the young Oyinbra was dealt with by the people she trusted the most. She also appealed that the baby be given to a couple with fairly grown children of their own.

Perefadei's life style changed as a result of her experiences with Ebisine and her subsequent guardianship of Oyinbra. She became an activist and joined a non-governmental organization (NGO) dedicated to tackling children's issues, particularly creating awareness in the area of sexual harassment and abuse. She was fond of 'talking' to Oyinbra about her new area of interest, always beginning her conversations with,

"Little one, we must expose men who take delight in raping and molesting children. They walk with the devil and must not be given the opportunity to spread their poison. Whether they are artisans like the ones who raped you or family or friends, they must be exposed and jailed. I know your spirit is working with us my beloved Oyinbra. You have a beautiful baby girl and I will make sure she is well cared for. Talking to you like this always increases my determination and I thank you," Perefadei would usually conclude.

Meanwhile, Ebisine and Nemi were compelled to sue the community health centre. A couple whose child was also born same night as their son Powei, brought an action against the health centre which affected Ebisine. Trouble started when the couple's child was diagnosed with a genetic ailment. Investigations showed an absence of the said disease in neither family of the child. The baffled parents went to the health centre in search of answers and could not believe what they discovered. Their child was given to another couple! Switched at birth! Naturally, they wanted their true child back!

"What do you mean it is such a long time so we should just carry on with our lives and try to make the best of a bad situation?" they shouted at the matron in charge.

"If somebody took our child from this health centre, it is your fault and we want our child back immediately. We don't care how you go about it. Just produce our child!" demanded the angry parents.

"Please take it easy," pleaded the now visibly anxious matron.

"We have a record of all the women that gave birth that night. Please be rest assured that a proper identification will be made." the matron pleaded.

The health centre immediately contacted all the relevant families. In the final analysis, it turned out that Ebisine's 'child' actually belonged to another woman. After several meetings and mediations by traditional rulers of the affected families' communities, the children were exchanged. Ebisine's true son was handsome and tall for his age. Nemi and his wife were quite happy with the boy's looks. However, happiness turned to horror when they were told that he had an incurable disease. He was expected to become completely bedridden in less than a year.

To make their cup of unhappiness full, Ebisine's doctor told her that she would be unable to conceive again. The venereal disease her husband was treated for had caused irreversible damage to both of them. Ebisine was now barren, while Nemi had become sterile.

GLOSSARY

Apoo!	:	Exclamation of surprise or wonder.
Warenemi-esomo	:	Pre-engagement visit to bride's family.

THE SWIMMING HEAD

Endiama was an active town. Its citizens spoke in loud voices. Everyone busily got involved in one form of activity or the other. There was hardly any idle hands and crime was limited to occasional pilfering. Most adults were engaged in trading and other commercial activities, while the young ones mostly concerned themselves with fishing, farming, hunting and wrestling. Though this modest town of about one thousand souls could not be described as wealthy, the inhabitants considered themselves better-off than most of their neighbours. They respected themselves and were inordinately proud of their heritage. It was common to hear the popular self-acclamatory shout.

"Endiama bolobolo ebigbo. Ebitimifa! Ebitimifa! Ebitiimifa! Yeei Yoo!" This was repeated with pride, at both private and public functions. This according to the elders was a morale booster meant to remind Endiama citizens of their greatness. Not even a young child was allowed to feel inferior in the presence of strangers from any of the bigger communities.

"Greet the visitor properly and don't forget to beat your chest, exclaiming *Endiama gidigidi!*" the child would be advised.

Endiama was well respected by its neighbours who did not hesitate to consult them on a variety of issues, ranging from inter-communal treaties to paternity disputes. As the community evolved over the years, a leading house or family known as EBIEBI WARE emerged. Their rise to prominence was credited to the superior abilities of the lineage's progenitors to lead the community effectively. Successive members earned respect by selflessly giving to the whole town, what others would rather

116

reserve for themselves or their immediate families. They also fought wars and took risks on behalf of their people. Since they were fearless, majority of inhabitants were only too happy to queue behind them. With the above scenario, it was predictable therefore that the Ebiebi family would one day become the community's rock and thereby assume leadership of Endiama. When the town got itself entangled in some legal web, an Ebiebi family member would be there to bear, not only the cost of litigation but put up appearance and mobilize others to do same. The patriarch of this family, EKEKAI was fond of admonishing his children and grandchildren to continue to walk in the path of honour, which had served the family so well over the ages.

"My children," he would say in his booming voice.

"Like many of my ancestors before me, I have become the pillar of this community because I risk my life without fear of losing it. Some may think I am a fool for doing this but I disagree. *Temearau* has blessed and prospered me beyond expectation. Look at you my children and grandchildren. Are you all not doing well or at least applying yourselves creditably well? What about my businesses? Am I not doing very well? Don't I give my wives whatever they want even at this old age? How many of my contemporaries in this Endiama can boast of doing the same eh, eh?"

Everyone agreed that the was right on all counts. Teitei, a beloved daughter, usually spoke on behalf of her siblings if the discussion was serious and formal.

"Daada, we will endeavour to follow your example all the time. Many people already envy us because of your stature in this community. They feel we are proud. Can the peacock help but spread its beautiful wings and raise its flamboyantly colourful tail? We cherish our rich heritage and do not hide this fact. Daada, thank you for always pointing us in the right direction, we are very grateful and will always cherish these intimate moments."

"Ehn, don't mind those lazy people my daughter. The lazy man's cry is always cantered on the invisible enemy. I cannot get tired of advising you.

My pride is you and my joy is also you, my beloved children, who will carry on the Ebiebi legacy long after I am gone." Ekikai would respond gruffly.

The Ebiebi family elders had the foresight to send their children to school at a time many people considered western education irrelevant and downright alien. This family was the first to interact with white traders who visited the area. The inhabitants of Endiama and their neighbours exhibited a mixture of excitement and uncertainty when the *Penaotu* appeared in the coastal region. The colour of the white men's skin was amazing to the people who originally mistook them for *oruama*, bent on invading and possibly wiping them off the face of the earth.

After this initial 'misunderstanding' however, the coastal people's eyes 'opened' and they did serious business with the white men. The Ebiebi family naturally or should we say expectedly, produced the first interpreters. They also built the first ever corrugated roofing sheets alias 'zinc' house in the entire clan. This was due in part, to the huge profits made through their new 'friends.'

It was the same Ebiebi family that produced the first London-trained graduate in the while clan. Not a too surprising feat some might say.

On one occasion, when the whole ethnic nationality, represented by all ten autonomous clans *oyia-ebe,* were invited to an all-night *agene* fiesta, an illustrious son of Ebiebi family who had come home with the fabled golden fleece was formally presented to the citizens. The family *bebeare-owi,* kakeagbe, made the introduction in a loud and penetrating voice.

"*Aaan Endiama! Eeen Endiama! Haan Oyia-ebe!*" Everyone enthusiastically responded.

"*Yiin!*"

"I, Kakeagbe, the cold water that burns, now speak as mandated by my kith and kin. I present to you the good and strong people of Endiama and Oyiaebe, our illustrious son Fun-ongbe. He flew to the white man's land in broad daylight! Mark this well my people. He flew to the land of bounty in the brightness of the sun, not like some who hide under or on top of trees in the dark, flying to suck the blood of the innocent! We know them and we see them getting poorer every day. We shall get them soon! *Haaan Oyiaebe!*" The gathering thundered a deafening.

'*Yiiin-aa!* Tell us more Kakeagbe of the people," they urged.

"As I was saying, our dear son Fun-ongbe, flew to the land full of glittering houses and snatched a big certificate, a thing unheard of in the days of our ancestors. He is now a big and important man, working with big people in the city. This is a very happy day, not only for us, his immediate family but the entire Oyiaebe. Proud Oyiaebe! I present to you the white feather in Ebiebi's cap, the golden cup of Endiama, Fun-ongbe!"

"*Yeeei Yeehh!*" hailed the crowd as Fun-ongbe was ushered into the arena surrounded by beautiful dancing girls.

"Speak to us Fun-ongbe," the people demanded.

Seeing that everyone waited expectantly, he had no choice but hide his shyness in a broad wave.

"My elders and people I greet you," he began.

"From the bottom of my heart I thank you for this great reception. I promise not to forget you or my roots. My heritage will definitely be a constant reminder that failure can never be permitted in my life. Let me seize this opportunity to tell all the young boys and girls of Endiama and Oyiaebe at large that you all have the ability to achieve whatever you want in life. Do not think that I am special. After all, was I the most brilliant in our class? The answer is a big NO! The only difference between me and some of my classmates was that even when I failed and did not get promoted to the next class, I did not give up. I was also not ashamed to repeat a class. In fact, repeating a class always made me work extra hard. That has been my philosophy of life and I am glad to share it with you. Once again, I thank you sincerely for this wonderful welcome. Gr-e-a-t Oyiaebe! I greet you all." He concluded.

There was thunderous applause. People excitedly discussed Fun-ongbe's speech as they laughed, sang and danced all night long. The story of the great feast is still told today, to the delight and amazement of the younger generation who do not have the opportunity of experiencing these ancient festivals any more.

The Ebiebi daughters many noted, were spectacularly successful in business. They were so gifted and talented that their nickname '*Golugolu*' was synonymous with wealth and power, which caused them to be admired by many and envied by a few. They were however respected by all.

This was the situation in Endiama when a distant cousin of Teitei of Ebiebi family, came to visit her. The visitor named Akpoa, was a simple looking man who told anyone who cared to listen, that he was once a rich man with four wives. He also claimed that it was the open and deadly display of witchcraft by his youngest wife Kolokolo-ere that reduced him to penury. Kolokolo-ere was the most beautiful girl in town and suitors flocked from far and near to seek her hand in marriage. Her refusal to marry any of the suitors fuelled a rumour that she was married to the fearsome groom of the river, Benikrukru. She was also said to be a senior spiritual daughter of the great witch and high priestess, Dirikii. All these speculations did not deter young bachelors from working hard to win her love, he alleged.

"Hmm! I was known to be a master chaser. No lady escaped my clutches if I was determined enough to go after her with my basketful of tricks. Honestly speaking, I was not interested in Kolokolo-ere because of all the chilling stories I had heard about her. Then one day, some friends dared me, even going as far as placing bets! They assured me that the young lady will reject me as she had rejected all the others. For the first time in my life, I was faced with the shameful possibility of having my advances turned down. Me, the open jaws of the crocodile! How could I have taken this challenge lying low my people?" he asked his listeners. Expecting no answer since everyone was just listening with rapt attention, he continued.

"I put everything into wooing the young woman. In all honesty, I only wanted to conquer her to prove to my friends that I still had power over women. But to my horror, she fell deeply in love with me! To make matters worse, she also succeeded in capturing my heart! Kolokolo-ere completely bewitched me and I became her slave, slave of love. Under the circumstances, a permanent union between us became inevitable. The long and short of it is that I ended up marrying her. All my friends and her numerous suitors were amazed at this development."

"Living with this beautiful woman was sheer heaven. Everything was going so well that I called her my 'magic mirror.' Patronage intensified whenever I sent her to any of my trading camps. Indeed, business was at its peak and money was no longer a problem for me. I naturally showered her with presents and she understandably became my favourite wife. The older wives became jealous and ganged up and picked fights with her from time to time. Gradually, things started changing economically. I noticed a steady slowing down in the business, which got progressively worse as time went on…."

"What did you do when your business started failing?" One listener asked, interrupting him.

"O! I contacted Odede'oru the great but things did not improve," he answered.

He went further to say that all his wives, including Kolokolo-ere deserted him after his properties mysteriously disappeared into other peoples' estates. Creditors that had forgiven him also suddenly came back to demand the long-forgotten debts. He was seriously harassed and threatened. Indeed, his life was in danger and he had no other choice than to leave his beloved home. He blamed his misfortunes on Kolokolo-ere. He felt that there was no other explanation for his sudden retrogression. Men committed suicide for less traumatic reasons and he was tempted at times to follow this part but always restrained himself because he was a man of faith.

In line with this faith, Akpoa fortunately remembered Teitei his prosperous distant cousin in Endiama. He decided to travel immediately to meet her. In light of all that had happened to him, Akpoa had no choice than to appeal to Teitei for help. He wanted her to re-establish him in business and also find him a young and industrious wife. She listened to this little known distant cousin's request without emotion, recalling that her late mother occasionally mentioned his name as the oldest son of her grandmother's first daughter Kesi. Teitei also remembered the pride in her mother's voice when news of Akpoa's wealth got to Endiama. With all these thoughts going through her mind, there was only slight irritation in her voice, when she responded to his appeal.

"Look Akpoa," She began.

"How can I render you this assistance when I do not even know you well? Granted that my late mother told me some stories about you and your mother. She was very excited danced when news of your rising profile reached her. Er..that is still no reason to make such a demand. I honestly think you are asking too much of me. Imagine! I should lend you money to trade and marry a wife for you as well! *Aboo*! Do I look like a mami-water to you?" she questioned.

Seeing that he was not making the desired impact on his cousin Akpoa, he resorted to pleading.

"*Aboo! Bene-arau*! Please have pity on me. you are my only hope. Think of how happy your dear mother would be if she was alive. She would have been proud that her grandmother's people decided to come close to you, her beloved daughter. I promise not to disappoint you. I will surprise you. I am very hard working and in no time at all, your investment will yield fruit," he assured her.

Teitei's soft and compassionate nature eventually gained upper hand and neutralized her objections. Akpoa's strong appeal to her emotions had worked.

"Akpoa, I pray that you do not go back on your words. Remember your sacred oath and don't forget that the ancestors watch our every step," she warned.

They then settled on modalities for repayment of the loan and a few other things. Akpoa was understandably very emotional and displayed the usual signs of happiness.

"I will never forget this," he swore, kneeling at Teitei's feet.

"May all our ancestors forever keep you in their sights," he prayed.

"You will never regret this," he further stated with emphasis and solemnly invoked the souls of their two mothers to bless and protect Teitei.

Teitei's first task was to start Akpoa off in gin trade, so she provided him with five *sangos* of gin and one hundred shillings. The loan was to be repaid over a period of five years and since no interest was being charged, they agreed that Akpoa should assist at Teitei's farm, once every market week. Akpoa's acceptance of this arrangement was enthusiastic. The business aspect concluded, Teitei now started looking around for a suitable wife. Akpoa had now become quite attached to her. Before long, a pretty and enterprising young woman was found.

When teitei broke the happy news about the prospective bride, Akpoa was so excited that he carried her shoulder high, calling on the gods of land and sea to bless and protect her. On the day of the marriage, Teitei donated her camp house to the lucky husband and wife. She promised not to pressure them to build their own. Indeed, they were to live in the camp house indefinitely. Akpoa could hardly contain his joy. He couldn't help but gloat and wag his finger at his invisible former favourite wife Kolokolo-ere.

"You witch, make sure you don't look in my direction again-o! I will not allow you spoil things for me this time around. Don't think you can extend your evil hands through any quarters whatsoever! I will surely wipe out anybody who attempts to pull me down. Be warned!" he would conclude darkly, shaking his head as if to clear it of fog or cobwebs.

It looked as though Kolokolo-ere never quite left his consciousness because he was known to mumble and call out her name even while in the midst of people. As a matter of fact, some persons considered him a bit queer and preferred to avoid his company. There were others however, who tickled him for stories about his so-called youthful adventures. Several jokes circulated at his expense, though he appeared oblivious to such goings on.

The years rolled by quickly and it came time for Akpoa to pay back the loan. Teitei herself felt confident that her cousin would not wait to be reminded before paying up. In fact, unknown to Akpoa, she had decided to give a third of the amount to his wife to start a business, as soon as he repaid her in full. This secret desire of hers made Teitei all the more anxious for a quick redemption of the debt. She knew from experience that the best way to keep a young wife happy was to set her up in any business of her choice so that she could have some independence. Another benefit comes in the area of home maintenance and welfare of the children. A woman with a business had no reason to run to her husband for basic day-to-day needs. She would also be in a position to buy decent clothes and make her husband proud by wearing such at festivals.

One full year after the due date, Akpoa was yet to repay the loan. This delay troubled Teitei greatly and she casually mentioned it to Akpoa's wife. As it turned out, the response from Mrs. Akpoa caused her more concern than calm.

"My husband has been grumbling about some wicked people who want to ruin him again. He said he has been having bad dreams and one particular face keeps pursuing him with a cutlass." She paused briefly.

"My dear in-law, you won't believe it but my husband said it is your face that he sees chasing him with a cutlass all the time!"

"Heyyy! Heaven forbid!" Teitei hissed.

"I hope your husband's senses are still with him or has he made friends with some destructive elements who are leading him astray? What nonsense! I, Teitei pursue him with cutlass! What for ehn? Look…"

"I know." Mrs. Akpoa cut in.

"Please do not be angry. I would not have bothered to tell you if you hadn't come by today. Surely, you, his benefactress cannot plan evil against him! I personally think he is not in a right frame of mind. His alcoholism must be having a serious impact on his thinking. Do you know that he comes home drunk most nights? I am very worried Teitei, please help us. Just last night, he suddenly woke up in the middle of the night screaming.

"Kolokolo-ere! Kolokolo-ere! Have you come back to join them?"

"Can you imagine? I'm really afraid-o!" she sighed heavily.

Though the disturbing conversation she had with Akpoa's wife weighed heavily on her mind, Teitei had no choice but to reluctantly invite Akpoa and ask for her money. Unable to look her in the eye, he mumbled some incoherent excuses, promising to repay the loan in the shortest possible time. He begged and cried and promised some more. Sadly, Teitei realized that it would be difficult to recover her money, so she invited the elders to intervene.

After everyone got seated, Teitei addressed them.

"Elders of Endiama, I have called you out of your houses to this *etele* because of Akpoa's refusal to honour our agreement. He is proving to be an ungrateful relative. For the sake of our two departed mothers, I do not want to make trouble with him. My fathers and mothers please, take this bottle of gin for the inconvenience of calling you out to settle this matter."

Elder Beke pointed his snuff stained index finger at Akpoa and commanded him to make his defence with a word of caution.

"Foolish excuses will not be entertained. Imagine a full-grown man behaving like those senseless little boys. *Kiman!* Put down a bottle of gin quick and speak up!" he ordered.

"My good elders," began Akpoa in a quaky voice.

"This is the gin. I have no excuse. Please beg Teitei for me. She has been so good to me and I am ashamed of what has happened. I promise to repay in instalments and in five markets, I should complete the payment," he begged, tears trickling down his cheeks.

All assembled concluded that the man was truly sorry. They rose and warned him to repay without fail, while appealing to Teitei to give him one more chance. The elders called Akpoa aside shortly after the meeting and warned him again to repay the loan or face severe sanctions.

As Akpoa left the *etele*, he frowned in frustration, murmuring and grumbling to himself.

"I must find a way out of this shame. All these things must be the handiwork of witches. After all, I do not waste the little money I am making on useless things. I only use the money on women and a few drinks from time to time. The women are not even demanding, with the exception of that divorcee *Gbaa*. *Temearau*! What a woman! She is so beautiful, so sweet and stubborn. All my friends have tasted divorcees so I must also have this one! I don't care how much I spend," he vowed.

He was apparently more concerned with keeping up appearances as a macho man than settling his indebtedness. Unknown to Teitei, the man was actually annoyed with her for dragging him before the elders. He considered the whole thing a great humiliation and hissed and sighed whenever he remembered the way the spokesman rudely asked him to respond. The hurt he felt was almost physical. Not only did his heart beat faster, his sight also blurred a little. The disgrace notwithstanding, he carried on his life with the usual laxity and predictably, he was unable to meet the numerous deadlines imposed by himself and the elders.

It got to the point where even his wife threatened to leave him if he refused to repay her beloved benefactress. Endiama hummed with the man's ingratitude. Baleful stares met him at every turn. The debt was now over three years overdue. People wanted to know what Akpoa was doing with his money. Speculations were rife. Some hinted that he was in fact the son of a water goddess, who demanded that all monies he earned be given to her. Others swore that he was merely pretending not to have money, while transferring huge sums to his ancestral home for stock-pilling. Guesses and more guesses but what was the truth? Only his allies and fellow womanizers knew the real reason for his inability to meet his financial obligations and they kept this information to themselves.

While all this was going on, Teitei went to her farm one day and did not return. This was strange because she was known to be punctual in returning after her farm work. Members of her household anxiously informed the elders and other notable people in the family. Not wanting to take chances, a search party was quickly put together. Agile and strong men armed with Dane guns, cutlasses and torches jumped into a few canoes and off they went, paddling furiously. As people familiar with their terrain, they wasted no time in combing the forest around Teitei's farm. The searchers fanned out to neighbouring farms and even creeks but did not see the woman or her canoe. The party returned at midnight, a bit dispirited but not discouraged. Early the next morning, they went out to continue the search. They returned at dusk, forlorn and sad. These were experienced hunters and farmers and many in the town expected them to find the missing woman. Some people started weeping openly, fearing the worst. In all this confusion, Akpoa was a pillar of encouragement, urging the people searching for Teitei not to despair. He did not join the searchers, claiming that as a non-indigene, he did not understand the layout of the farms and creeks. There were more competent persons to handle such matters and indeed they were already doing a good job as far as he was concerned. By the third day, everyone was more or less convinced that something terrible had happened to Teitei. There was much crying and lamentation. Akpoa and his wife cried the loudest.

The Ebiebi family consulted the main oracle of Endiama to know the fate of their sister. They promised to avenge her death, if indeed she had unfortunately died at the hands of some unscrupulous person or persons. The young people were restive and wanted to know the result of the divination immediately. The oracle's verdict was inconclusive. More consultations were needed for a more definitive pronouncement, said the chief priest. He sent word about a possible breakthrough in his divination and demanded for yet another big hen, a he-goat, a *sango* of gin and twelve shillings. Even before this request was met, there was pandemonium in the town.

There were shouts of Abomination! Abomination! Sounding from every direction and people ran helter-skelter to locate the direction or spot of the commotion.

At last, everyone converged at the waterfront to behold the most incredible, incomprehensible and baffling sight ever seen by a people! As all looked fixedly at the river, turning their heads this way and that, it became clear that a woman was swimming desperately. But what was totally unacceptable was that the woman looked like Teitei, was indeed Teitei! To put it more factually, Teitei's head! The head swam like crazy in front of the Ebiebi waterfront until a couple of brave men went in a canoe to collect it. Meanwhile, Akpoa had fainted at the sight of the swimming head. As consciousness returned, he started pulling out hairs from his head shouting,

"*Woo woo*! Teitei, how can you come back to life again? Get away quickly you hear me? Quickly, go away! *Woo woo*! Teitei, don't sprinkle blood into my eyes-o! People! This wicked woman is blinding me. Oh! Oh! Blood in my eyes! Head! Hands! Everywhere!"

He started removing his clothes and began washing his hands in empty space. Endiama people could not believe their ears and eyes. People swore at the now deranged Akpoa, freely invoking all the demons in hell to tackle him. Meanwhile, Akpoa collapsed as Teitei's head was carried ashore, letting out a blood-cuddling scream as he gasped and died. His dead body was spat on, trampled on and finally thrown into the river for fishes to feast on.

<u>GLOSSARY</u>

Endiama	-	*Fish town*
Bolobolo	-	*The first*
Ebiogbo	-	*Goodland*
Ebitimfa	-	*Remain good forever*
Yeei	-	*Social greeting at a gathering*
Yoo	-	*Response to the greeting*
Endiamarians	-	*Fish town citizens*
Ebiebi	-	*Good-good*
Teitei	-	*Always escaping*
Daada	-	*Father*
Ehn	-	*Exclamation*
Pena-otu	-	*White people*
Oyia-ebe	-	*Ten clans*
Bebe-are-owei	-	*Spokesman*
Kake-agbe	-	*Mature age fits*
Aaan	-	*Solidarity greeting at gatherings*
Eeen	-	*Response to the greeting*
Yiin	-	*Also response to solidarity greeting*
Fun-ongbe	-	*Book champion*
Yiiiin-aa	-	*Response to solidarity greeting*
Golugolu	-	*As priceless as gold*
Akpoa	-	*Lamentation*
Kolokolo-ere	-	*Bitter woman*
Kesi	-	*Petit*
Mami	-	*Water goddess*
Aboo	-	*Exclamation of surprise*
Bene-arou	-	*Sister*
Gidigidi	-	*Expression of greatness*
Sangos	-	*Glass gin containers*
Temearau	-	*Creator/Mother God*

Etele	-	*Village resting place/Also an open house for gathering, built on stills*
Beke-	-	*English*
Kiman!	-	*A slang for hurry up*
Woowoo!	-	*Shout of fright/delight*
Dirikii	-	*Darkness or denseness*

THE DOG

"Tupele! Tupele! Stop running around with that red-eyed dirty dog and wash the plates. Do you hear me?"

"Alright Mama," responded Tupele, speeding off to the sandbank, almost breaking one of his mother's precious 'breaking plates' stacked by the water's edge for him to wash. Osuo, Tupele's mother could not contain herself anymore and charged at her son, whip in hand.

"You foolish idiot," she abused, as the whip descended on his back. The boy screamed in pain and dodged as he saw his mother raise the whip for another lash.

"So, you want to break my plates hnn? Then I will use money meant for other things to buy another set so that those Onitsha traders who are already rich will get richer, while I become poorer eh? When will 'play, play' leave this your coconut head, you Tupele, tell me!" she screamed, giving him a conk on the head.

Meanwhile Tupele's dog Kposa, did not find the harassment of his master funny and barked at Osuo, who glared threatening at it. She left her son and his dog but not without a parting shot.

"Know that I am going to use the big deep 'breaking plate' for your uncle's soup this afternoon, so hurry up-o!" Realizing that Tupele was barely paying attention, she shouted.

"Tupele! Did you hear me, eh!.................."

"Yes Mama, I heard you very well and Kposa too heard you," he laughed, stroking the dog's head. Osuo looked at him sternly and walked away. Kissing Kposa's nose tenderly, Tupele whispered,

"Mama is a wonderful mother really, my boy. Even when she is upset, you can see the love in her eyes. She has told me many times that I have a chance of becoming the first millionaire in this village. What do you think my boy?" Kposa dutifully wagged his tail in agreement. Tupele parted the dog lovingly and smiled.

"I knew you would agree with her. Even a dog knows the advantage of being a millionaire's pet. No more scrambling for excrements and leftovers with every other dog in town! Pray my ambitious one, that we achieve our dream." The dog wagged its tail vigorously and looked up at its master intently. Tupele laughed merrily.

"I fully expect you to contribute your quota towards actualizing this vision by praying hard. Ehn! Who says dogs don't pray? If you think yours is to sit pretty and enjoy imported dog meals, you better think again!" So saying, he threw Kposa into the river for a hearty swim.

Tupelo joined the dog and they had such a good time that he almost forgot his mother's admonition but for the timely appearance of his sister, Funemi-ere which quickly brought him back to the task at hand. He swam ashore, put the plates into the wash basket and ran home with the now clean, invigorated and happy Kposa following closely behind. Fortunately for him, his mother had not finished preparing her special *okorien fulou* by the time he got home. Happy that he completed his task on time, she rewarded him with a big smile and promise of a plate of her special delicacy.

Tupelo's father Tikotiko, a court clerk, had just returned from work and overheard his wife make the promise to her son.

"Well, well, Mama Tupele, did I hear you bribing my son?" he queried in mock seriousness, frowning for effect. He looked from mother to son and all bust out laughing.

"Hey! It is not a laughing matter. I am going to *somos* you if you do not answer my question, wife or no wife, law is law!"

"Ah my husband," Osuo laughed.

"Tupele proved me wrong today. You know how playful he has become since you bought him that dog. Frankly, this issue of the dog has to be revisited because he is becoming too attached to the animal......"

"Please," Tikotiko cut in.

"Let's not go into the dog matter again my dear wife, I beg you. Please be patient with the boy. Now tell me about the bribe, na!" Nodding, she continued.

"I caught him running around with the dog, leaving the dirty aluminium plates unwashed. I flogged him only once and warned him to wash and bring the plates to me without breaking my precious 'breaking plates.' Surprisingly, he not only did as I asked but came home earlier than expected."

Tikotiko was happy and clapped delightedly.

"Mama Tupele," he beamed.

"This boy will become somebody tomorrow. Mark my words! It will not surprise me if he becomes one of the most important young men in this village. Mark my words! My son is a potential millionaire. Come Tupele and shake my hand!" he demanded.

The excited young man solemnly stretched out his hand for a firm handshake while faithful Kposa shared in the excitement by jumping up and licking his master all over the body. Tupele was about ten years old when the above incident took place and it left a lasting impression on him.

At that age, Tupele like many young children in the various riverine communities, was just in primary two. Many city dwellers may not understand how or why a ten-year-old should be in primary two, when many city children of that age would already be in junior secondary school. Who will blame them for not comprehending the situation? Well, let us leave that for another time. Suffice to say the reality of the Niger Delta village child which Tupele is, is radically different from the city child's. They are akin to the proverbial parallel lines that cannot be meet.

Basic amenities like pipe borne water, electricity, paved roads, television, telephone, yes and even the magical Global System for Mobile communication 'GSM' now taken for granted by city children all spell one word, **FOREIGN** to Tupele and his friends, as space ships were to city youngsters fify or so years ago!

Since Tupele and everyone else freely defecate in the river from which they fetch their drinking water, no one needs a soothsayer to conclude that water borne diseases equally visited them freely. Cholera and its brothers, sisters, parents and grandparents paid frequent uninvited house calls on Tupele's family as well as other families. These dangerous visitors usually left in their trail, death and sorrow. The families, in all fairness fight back with herbs and roots, incantations and spells, charms and amulets and in recent times, with expired drugs sold by itinerant hawkers and resident patent medicine dealers without license, naturally. As can be imagined, children in Tupele's community of Aya and other such villagers experienced stunted growth, which is why, Tupele, though ten years old, was no taller than a typical six-year old city child. However, their environment notwithstanding, when Tupele and his friends played hard. They exhibited the robust carefree laughter of children everywhere. The children enjoyed playing on the wide sandbanks, exotic looking creeks and rivers. Endless wakes were also a source of regular entertainment. Now, let's talk about these funerals a little bit.

These were particularly fun-filled for most children, not only because of the exciting *owigiri* music but also the free drinks and food which they have to scramble for. Little wonder then that instead of being frightened at the site of a dead body, Tupele and his friends were usually thrilled at the prospect of looking one squally in the face! They take advantage of their little sizes to take up the best viewing positions as a body lay in state. It was common for these children to debate the beauty or otherwise of the various coffins bodies were buried in and even the appearance(s) of the corpse(s)! Since parents did not bother to enforce sleeping hours, children could stay up as late as twelve midnight or beyond. What with the daily grind of fishing, farming, trading and feeding as many as twenty mouths or is it stomachs? The last thing on the minds of these hassled and frazzled parents was the time a child went to bed!

"Were we ever pampered by our parents when we were young?" They would snap if questioned about their attitude.

"You people from the city really have strange ideas. Why on earth will I police my children? Do you know how many children I have?" A flustered father would ask.

"Do you want me to die before my time? *Aboo*! Please let us discuss more important things," he would tersely advise. The picture painted above was the typical the world of Tupele and his parents.

When Tupele was about twelve years old, he was stricken by a strange illness. His frantic parents consulted all the known oracles and deities, to no avail. Several traditional healers were consulted and these duly administered their herbs and roots but the poor boy made no progress, in fact his condition continued to deteriorate. In desperation, Osuo and Tikotiko joined a vision seeing church in the hope that their faith would be built up, thereby attracting spiritual healing for their son. Fasting and praying was recommended and the duo enthusiastically complied. Tupele was taken to the church for overnight stays amidst serious and continues prayers, drumming, dancing and singing. Yet, his health steadily grew worse. He was in terrible pain and movement became impossible. The once vibrant and carefree young boy was now bedridden. As weeks stretched into months, Osuo and Tikokiko daily cried in each other's arms in the privacy of their bedroom.

The thought of losing their dear son was so unbearable that they became zombie-like even as other areas of worry also came up at this time. Osuo's income, which used to be substantial, had virtually dried up. Tikotiko's pittance of a salary could no longer sustain the family. The distressed family found themselves in an intolerable situation. What were their options now? How much longer could Tupele hang on to life? An important question was who to borrow money from to ease things a little? Another question was even if they miraculously found such a creditor, could they accommodate the usual compound interest charged? But above all, since Tupele was almost embracing death, did it make sense to incur any debt? Tikotiko and Osuo, being pragmatists and realists concluded that it was not worth the effort and braced up for the inevitable. Tupelo would surely die whether they borrowed money or not, so why bother? There would be no future millionaire to make their family great, they lamented.

As Tupele lay dying, only one soul still had any shred of hope left, it seemed. This soul was Kposa the faithful dog, which became more alert as its master grew weaker. The news of Tupele's imminent death threw the little community into mourning. Relatives and friends kept vigil in his room, which had a sombre atmosphere as people spoke in whispers. There were also occasional sobs.

Then suddenly, Kposa who had been agitated for some time, leapt onto the dying boy's bed and bit him twice on the stomach, one bite on either side! Blood gushed from the wounds and confusion reigned as many hands tried to stop the bleeding, at the same time! Others rushed to remove the blood-stained bed sheet. In the frenzy that followed, no one paid much attention on the dog.

All attention was fixed on Tupele who had miraculously recovered! He quickly rose from his bed as if from a deep and refreshing sleep. The young man's inexplicable and sudden recovery was nonetheless greeted with spontaneous jubilation. Wild speculations and postulations trailed the bizarre behaviour of Kposa. What really was Kposa? Was it a real dog? Was it a spirit? Was it a guardian angel? Questions and more questions. First thing the next morning, Tupele called out to Kposa in his usual manner. He whistled repeatedly but there was no responding bark. Surprised, he went to the front yard. His shrill shout woke up the household. They ran out to the front yard and saw Tupele lying face down next to Kposa. The family quickly revived their son, whose face was wet with tears mixed with sand. The cause of Tupele's grief was later identified as his weeping increased and all attempts to calm him failed. Kposa the faithful dog lay dead, its busy body stiff, eyes wide open. The entire Aya community trooped out to give Kposa a hero's burial, a conduct unheard off in the history of the village. Tupelo lived to be an old man and never forgot his cherished dog, Kposa.

FOOTNOTES

Breaking Plates - Slang for Ceramics dishes.
Okorien Fulou[2] - Soup prepared with breadfruit
Somos[3] - Corruption of the word summon
Aboo[4] - Exclamation of irritation or surprise

THE HAND OF THE DEAD

My name is Boye, a young boy of sixteen. I have always lived with my parents in our town, Ama. The main occupation of our people is gin brewing because we are surrounded by wild raffia palm forests. Fishing and farming also occupy a lot of our time. Are you surprised that we also farm? Eeh! So, you are one of those who think that riverine people actually float merrily from place to place, doing everything on water? What gave you such an idea? I suggest you educate yourself by traveling to as many riverine towns and villages as possible. Please don't just drive to the waterfront of either of coastal cities and tell me you have visited a riverine town. That will not do at all! You must get on a boat or preferably a canoe and explore those beautiful waterways and marvel at nature's lavish display of wealth. More of this later. Remember, I was telling you about my town and our various occupations.

My father had about five tapping zones and one main brewing camp. The tapping zones are forest plots. Even though the zones and swamps, everyone knows and respects each other's boundaries. As a responsible son who planned to step into his father's shoes at the appropriate time, I accompanied him to tap wine and brew gin on many occasions. My father in turn, showed me all his plots. Some had matured palms, while others spotted young and maturing ones. One or two had completely yielded their juice and were now allowed to 'rest.' I learnt fast and in no time at all, found myself involved in tapping and brewing. This made my father proud because I was not like most of the young men who preferred to loaf around playing draughts or worse still, chasing little girls in the market place. The elders agreed with my father when he beat his chest and proclaimed often.

"*Temearau* has blessed me with a real man for a son. He will be a leader someday. Yes, my son is a man *Owei ke owei!*"

I must confess that at sixteen, I felt grown up inwardly and confident. I started listening to the elders' discussions at the town's square or the *etele*. Wisdom oozed from their mouths and this created a hunger in me to learn and know more about life. A particular old man called EBIKABOWEI singled me for special favour. This kind old man offered me a standing invitation to visit his hut once a week, precisely on the eve of Ama market.

Oh friends, I lack words to express my joy whenever I called on Pa Ebikabowei. My whole being would be wrapped in pure happiness for as long as I remained with him and afterwards, my feet would feel so light as I walked home that I could confidently say that I am usually close to flying! You could say that what effectively prevented me from leaping and flying into the sky, was the fear of being called a wizard! You know how our people are, if you murmur to yourself, you are a suspect. A continuously bent head, were the person is busy looking at the ground while walking, causes great concern and the witch catcher is usually informed, for necessary action! You now understand why my joy had to be contained within my heart and soul, with my feet firmly planted on the ground but need I tell you that the tutelage consisted of deep spiritual truths, timeless and enduring in nature? You already guessed it? Great!

Pa Ebikabowei's lessons were both thrilling and frightening. How so when I earlier said I was joyful? Simple, the way of life expected of a person interested in following the teachings strictly is the reason for my statement. I know this sounds paradoxical but it is the only way I can describe it. My mentor, as I prefer to call Pa Ebikabowei, taught in simple way. He narrowed everything to the power of THOUGHT. He explained that those who have strayed into darkness are good souls horrifically deceived by their own emotions. According to my mentor, these people's lives then become entwined in a lethal web that covers EVERYTHING they do. Think about it. What causes anxiety, greed, anger, pride, insecurity, superiority complex, inferiority complex and many such 'negatives?' If you carefully examine the causes of these traits, you will discover that fear, deep rooted fear is the culprit. Fear of discovery of his/her emptiness is a great incentive for pride's head to be raised sky-high. On the other hand, the insecure person is griped by a fear of dispossession by asking, "What if I lose my position, what if my secret is leaked by that ungrateful fellow? What if people discover that I paid that rascal to write my final paper? What if my parishioners find out that I am a rapist?" What if and what if? The questions are endless for the fear filled candidate of insecurity.

Is it not amazing that superiority and inferiority complex holders source their fear from one and the same parent? The superior person has the illusion of being so high up in the social, intellectual and economic ladder that he/she is in constant fear of reality's dawn, which has a peculiar way of exposing inadequacies. By the same token, the inferior fellow is also griped by the illusion that everyone else is sprinting or has sprinted past them in the social, intellectual and economic arenas. Both groups fear the responsibility exposure will place on them. Do you think I have made a strong case to support my opinion as taught by my mentor that FEAR is fatal to those who are in its grasp? Have, I also expressed Pa Ebikabowei's teachings correctly that our lives are structured according to our THOUGHTS? If your answer to both questions is a big YES, then I'm glad but if not, I must then go back to him for more tutorials, this time on the art of elucidation.

I must tell you that as I eagerly anticipated my quality time with my mentor on the eve of every market, I could not help thinking about how best to spend my adult life. The old man was unlocking several aspects of my consciousness which hitherto blissfully slumbered. I started questioning a lot of belief systems and even the way we were living. I was always pensive on the eve of my lessons because I would be literarily busting with questions to ask Pa Ebikabowei. The above scenario mirrored my situation when without warning, fate made a rude entrance into my corner of the world.

I was immediately catapulted to adulthood. Even though my biological age was only sixteen. How did I know this so exactly, you ask? You are right in asking and I will answer you. Though illiterate, my father's brain was 'fire!' His native intelligence was so high that the villagers nicknamed him *"Agbereke or Gbregbre."* He correctly calculated dates by watching and noting nature's signs and signals in the tide, how certain birds flew in and out of the forests and the seasons. His ability to compute correctly was uncanny. Anyway, enough of the digression! I was telling you about now fate, uninvited, intruded into my world. On the day in question, my father went alone to one of his tapping sites. This was not unusual because he was a very strong person and did not demand or expect assistance all the time. The tappers' network was such that whenever anyone finished his work early, he would visit a colleague. So it was that Tuabowei paddled to my father's site late in the work day. According to him, the forest was abuzz with songs from humans and mammals and he felt at ease with himself. Sadly however, this feeling of ease evaporated the minute he saw the submerged canoe of my father. He paddled fast to the canoe and could not help letting out a big yell for help. My father had evidently fallen from the twenty odd feet high raffia palm tree and hit his head over the side of the canoe, which then capsized. He was lifeless when his friend found him. Tuabowei's continuous shouts brought fellow tappers to the scene and they tried to revive my father but to no avail. He was finally transported home and a wake was observed for him that night as demanded by custom.

I cannot describe my grief and utter confusion. I sincerely felt so lost that my sobs were barely audible. However, I had to be strong for my mother who was inconsolable and my junior siblings who were also wailing and throwing themselves on the ground. My father was buried the next day and it fell on me to quickly take charge of affairs. I recruited two men to take immediate control of the brewing camp and four of the tapping sites, while I took over the remaining one. I waited until the end of the mandatory seven days of mourning before resuming full business activities. As time went on, routine was established and I was able to take adequate care of my mother and siblings. Pa Ebikabowei proved to be a real mentor during this most distressing period of my life. For obvious reasons, I could no longer visit him regularly, so the times I now spent with him were even more precious.

Barely six months after the sudden transition of my father, I noticed an encroachment on one of the forest sites. A neighbour of my father's Bibo, decided to annex the site in question. Incidentally this man was considered to be one of the well-to-do men in our community and his arrogance was well known. I ran to Pa Ebikabowei, who then called the elders and briefed them. Thereafter, Bibo was summoned by the whole council of elders and leaders for a meeting. He dully obeyed the summons but insisted that the forest was his for keeps. He considered it an insult that a small boy like me dared to challenge him. He boasted that it was laughable that I was attempting what even my late father could never have contemplated. The elders were offended that Bibo refused to listen to them and warned him of the dire consequences that awaited him if he continued the forceful acquisition. Bibo laughed in their faces and dared anyone to try to stop him. When it became clear that the trespasser was more than determined to take over the forest completely, I faced him squarely and calmly told him under no circumstances must he, Bibo, enter my part of the tapping forest. I warned him to listen to the council of elders and respect their decision. So saying, I presented a bottle of traditional dry gin to the council and begged to be excused. My wish was granted and I left.

About a week after this meeting, I went back to the elders and told them that Bibo was now consolidating his hold on the forest by sending guest workers into the area for full-fledged tapping. I pleaded with the *Amanana owei*, who is the father of the entire town to appeal to Bibo. The *Amanana-owei*, being a compassionate and just ruler, acted on my request and asked his assistant to call a town meeting without delay, which he did. Bibo was asked to state why he blatantly disobeyed the council of elders. Disdain characterized his every word and the *Amanana-owei* could not believe his ears. As he made to get up to scold the rude Bibo, a hush fell on the crowd. No, it was not because they wanted to listen to the high chief, not at all. It was because my dear 'departed' father himself decided to show up, attired in his burial finery and addressed the gathering as follows.

"*Amanana-owei*, chiefs, elders and people of Ama, *ado*! My mission is a simple one. I have come to tell Bibo never to cross the boundary between our two forests. I am going back to my camp to stay. Any further incursion into my forest will lead to his death" So saying, he promptly vanished.

Need I tell you that goose bumps registered freely on all flesh or that many people took to their heels? The man Bibo was shivering so hard, I actually felt sorry for him. I thought he would pass out there and then but he managed to stagger out of the meeting venue. The meeting ended without the usual protocols. Of course, the incident formed the sole topic of discussion for a long time not only in our community but beyond. The conclusion of the people was incontestable. They agreed that the so-called dead definitely and unequivocally have a hand in the activities of the living.

What do you think? Please let me know, I can assure you that I no longer feel bereaved because my father lives, guiding and protecting us, his loved ones. Now that I understand, it makes perfect sense that life is a continuum a never-ending cycle of births, deaths, rests and births and deaths and rests.

Friends, this is the story of my life so far. Watch out for more exciting happenings in the future. I am certainly destined for an extraordinary life!

GLOSSARY

Ado!	-	*General Greeting*
Oweike owei	-	*A true man*
Amananaawei	-	*Traditional head of a town*
Agbreke/Gbregbre	-	*A person who speaks with confident and in an intelligent manner*
Temearau	-	*The Creator, mother God*

FATU AND THE TAIL
OF ELEPHANT

There was a man named Sawa, who was already very wealthy when he married his beautify wife, Fatu. Sawa was very impressed with the behaviour of his wife because she always treated him like a king. Fatu even inconvenienced herself to satisfy her husband's every wish. While most men would have remained contented and just enjoyed the adoration of their wife, Sawa was a bit unsettled about the woman's behaviour. In one breath, he doubted her sincerity, only to question himself the very next minute for mistrusting his wife's flawless treatment of him.

'What has come over me? instead of being happy, I am suspicions! Sawa, stop this nonsense!' he cautioned himself, at the same time shaking and beating his head with his left palm. However much he tried though, he could not stop himself from indulging in conspiracy theories about his own wife. In order to save himself from mental fatigue, he decided to act on his suspicions.

He dropped hints that the business front was becoming difficult and their life style would soon change, unless something dramatic happened. Fatu was naturally concerned and urged him not to give up but rather explore other types of businesses. Sawa promised to try harder but in fact, he continued to perfect his plan. Then one evening, Sawa announced to his stunned wife that he was almost broke. It dawned on Fatu then, that her lavish life style would soon come to a screeching halt. She was very unhappy at this development and grumbled.

"I have become accustomed to a rich life style. How can I cope without lots of money to satisfy my every need? O! What am I going to do?" she sighed heavily.

She found it intolerable to imagine that she could soon be compared to the struggling wives down the street, who were forced by economic realities to move from one bush market to another, hunting for bargains. Those women's faces were lined and wrinkled from stress and Fatu could not bear to think of herself looking that way in the not too distant future, if their financial situation remained dismal. She naturally blamed Sawa, her hitherto beloved husband for their predicament and it never occurred to her to salvage the mess by starting a small business of her own. No, never! Such thoughts were not allowed to mature in her head and were quickly banished when they attempted to pop up. As far as Fatu was concerned, it would be a big let-down, indeed a big shame for her to be seen engaging in petty trade. She, who was called madam and bowed to would now be jostling with these same people in mini-buses and rickety taxis or worse still, being baked by the harsh sun as she sat beside her wares in the market place.

"Oh! Simply unacceptable, unthinkable!" was Fatu's determined cry.

She became aggressive toward her husband and hissed and sighed ceaselessly, when Sawa told her that their finances had dried up completely. Fatu's sweet nature did a somersault. Food was now served with broken plates, carelessly place on the floor. Not for her erstwhile wealthy husband, the luxury of being served with shiny plates. Meanwhile, to complete his disguise, Sawa ensured that he only wore tattered clothes when going out in the mornings. This situation went on for quite a while until he became thoroughly fed up with Fatu's mistreatment. She treated him so atrociously that he took a musical instrument and started singing along the road.

"Bani fura demi ma ji you wan"

A wise old woman who heard Sawa singing called Fatu and told her about the man's song of lamentation, counselling her to burn the rags he usually wore. The old woman assured Fatu that burning the tattered clothes would cause him to assume his former condition. Fatu carried out the old woman's instructions to the letter and as predicted, Sawa reverted back to his original status. Seeing her husband in the old familiar state brought so much joy to Fatu that, she proceeded to prepare his favourite meal, complete with clean and shining plate settings. Sawa looked at his wife in amazement and bluntly refused to eat the food, telling her to pack out of his house. Fatu threw herself on the floor, begging and crying to be forgiven and given another chance but Sawa would not bulge.

"Why should I take you back when you have confirmed all my earlier suspicions and fears that you married me because of my wealth?" He questioned.

"Please Sawa, forgive and forget and let our marriage continue," Fatu pleaded.

"I behaved the way I did because of frustration, anger, fear and shame. My love for you is still strong and will last forever. If you refuse to take me back, I might consider suicide. Beloved *Sawa*, I cannot live without you," she wailed.

When the pleading was becoming unbearable for him, Sawa decided to give her what for him, was an impossible condition to fulfil before he would accept her back into his home.

The task he set for her looked dangerous, indeed even unattainable, at least to the ordinary person. So, what was it? The now 'love struck' Fatu was to produce the tail of an elephant! How about that? You would expect the distraught woman to wail and throw up her hands and beg for a less awesome assignment, right? Of course! Oh, not Fatu. She tied her wrapper firmly around her waist and nodded confidently.

"I will do as you ask my husband," was her unfazed response.

Moving quickly out of their compound, Fatu ran into a neighbour who had come to 'settle' the quarrelling couple because of the raised voices he overhead. She barely had time for a hello, before moving on. The neighbour was at a loss, wondering whether to continue on his mission or abandon it now that the woman was out of the house. He eventually decided to go on and at least let Sawa know his intention. Meanwhile, Fatu headed straight for her old woman adviser's humble dwelling. The woman was reclining peacefully on a wooden bench when she arrived. As was customary, Fatu knelt reverently and started picking out grey hairs from the old woman's head. After a few minutes and upon prompting, the story tumbled out in a rush from the anxious Fatu. Nodding, the wise old lady instructed as follows,

"Fill seven baskets with live flies and go deep into the forest where you will find a cave. Place the baskets carefully at the mouth of the cave where elephants could easily see and feed on them. Withdraw to a safe distance thereafter and act as unfolding events direct," the woman concluded.

Fatu hastened to find baskets, which she filled with flies and then went into the forest, following the old woman's directions until she saw a cave and placed the baskets as instructed and withdrew to a safe distance. Shortly thereafter, Fatu saw a huge elephant approaching the cave. The baskets full of flies, a known elephant delicacy must have been a pleasant surprise for the mother elephant who cautiously looked around. Satisfied that it was not a trap, it boldly walked towards the cave but stood at respectful distance to make assurance doubly sure that the whole thing was not a setup. Then, it sighted Fatu! Thereafter, a telepathic communication ensued. Upon positive confirmation that she meant no harm and was indeed the provider of the feast, mother elephant was so thrilled that it asked Fatu to make any request she may have. Not believing her luck, Fatu calmly made her appeal.

"What you want can be given to you," said the elephant.

"After all, I have many children who will be excited to feast on this banquet of flies and I can easily cut one of their tails for you before they even realize what is happening...."

Mother elephant was still speaking when her brood started arriving. They pounced on the flies and ate greedily, then filed into the cave, promptly falling asleep as they did. As promised, the tail of her last born was cut and given to Fatu, who ran with all her might until she got home. She then ceremoniously presented the coveted elephant tail to her astonished husband. He had no choice than to take her back. How about that! A promise is a promise you must agree! Fatu was not such a bad sort after all.

True? False? You be the judge.

GLOSSARY

Bani fura demi nna ji yon'won   -   *Give me millet drink because I'm hungry.*